BRIMSTONE

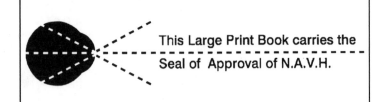

This Large Print Book carries the
Seal of Approval of N.A.V.H.

BRIMSTONE

ROBERT B. PARKER

LARGE PRINT PRESS
A part of Gale, Cengage Learning

GALE
CENGAGE Learning™

Detroit • New York • San Francisco • New Haven, Conn • Waterville, Maine • London

GALE
CENGAGE Learning™

LIBRARY OF CONGRESS CATALOGING-IN-PUBLICATION DATA

Parker, Robert B., 1932–
    Brimstone / by Robert B. Parker.
        p. cm. — (Wheeler Publishing large print hardcover)
    ISBN-13: 978-1-59722-995-1 (alk. paper)
    ISBN-10: 1-59722-995-4 (alk. paper)
        1. Large type books. I. Title.
PS3566.A686B75 2009b
813'.54—dc22   2009009951

ISBN 13: 978-1-59413-384-8 (pbk. : alk. paper)
ISBN 10: 1-59413-384-0 (pbk. : alk. paper)

Published in 2010 by arrangement with G. P. Putnam's Sons, a member of Penguin Group (USA) Inc.

Printed in the United States of America
1 2 3 4 5 6 7 14 13 12 11 10

For Joan:
Well worth the pressure

1

It's a long ride south through New Mexico and Texas, and it seems even longer when you stop in every run-down, aimless little dried-up town, looking for Allie French. By the time we got to Placido, Virgil Cole and I were almost a year out of Resolution.

It was a barren little place, west of Del Rio, near the Rio Grande, which had a railroad station, and one saloon for every man, woman, and child in town. We went into the grandest of them, a place called Los Lobos, and had a beer.

Los Lobos was decorated with wolf hides on the wall and a stuffed wolf behind the bar. Several people looked at Virgil when he came in. He wasn't special-looking. Sort of tall, wearing a black coat and a white shirt and a Colt with a white bone handle. But there was something about the way he walked and the way the gun seemed so natural. People looked at me sometimes, too, but always after they looked at Virgil.

"Think that wolf might've exprised of old age," Virgil said.

"A long time ago," I said.

"Exprised ain't right," Virgil said. "You went to West Point."

"Expired," I said.

"Means died," Virgil said.

"Uh-huh."

Virgil believed in self-improvement. He read a lot of books and had a bigger vocabulary than he knew how to use. He sipped his beer.

"Mexican," he said. "Mexicans know how to make beer."

"How much money you got?" I said.

"Got a dollar," Virgil said.

"More than I got," I said.

Virgil nodded.

"Guess we got to get some," he said.

I grinned at him.

"We got sort of a limited range of know-how," I said.

"Least we know it," Virgil said.

"Lotta saloons, lotta whores," I said. "Not much else."

"Railroad station," Cole said.

"Why?" I said.

"No idea," I said.

A tall, thin young man in an undershirt

8

stood up from a table near us and walked over to us. He wasn't heeled that I could see.

"Excuse me, sir," he said to Virgil. "Boys at my table got a bet. Some say you're Virgil Cole. Some say you're not."

The young man hadn't shaved lately, but he was too young to have much of a beard. His two front teeth were missing.

"I am," Virgil said.

The boy looked over his shoulder at the others at his table.

"See that?" he said. "See what I tole you?"

Everyone stared at Virgil.

"Seen you in Ellsworth," the kid said. "I was 'bout half growed up. Seen you kill two men slick as a whistle."

"Slick," Virgil said.

The others at his table were all turned toward us.

"How many men you figure you killed, Mr. Cole?"

"No need to count," Virgil said.

Most of the room was looking at us now, including the bartender. The boy seemed to have run out of things to say. Virgil was silent.

"Well, uh, it's been a real pleasure, Mr. Cole, to meet you. Can I shake your hand?"

"No," Virgil said.

The boy looked startled.

"Virgil don't shake hands," I said to the boy. "He don't see any good coming from letting somebody get hold of him."

"Oh," the boy said. "A'course not. I shoulda known."

Virgil didn't say anything. The boy backed away sort of awkwardly. When he got to his table, his friends gathered in tight and whispered together.

"No need to be explaining me," Virgil said to me.

"Hell there ain't," I said.

Virgil smiled. The kid at the next table got up and went out without looking at Virgil. A fat Mexican girl in a loose flowered dress came to the table.

"Good time for joo boys?" she said.

"Sit down," Virgil said.

"Buy drink?" she said.

Virgil shook his head.

"Nope," he said. "You know a woman named Allison French?"

The woman shook her head.

"Probably calls herself Allie?" Virgil said.

"No."

"Plays the piano?" Virgil said. "Sings?"

"Don't know nobody," the Mexican woman said. "Round the world for a dollar. Joo friend, too."

Virgil smiled.

"No," he said. "Thanks."

"No drink?" she said. "No fuck?"

"Nope," Virgil said. "Anybody knows Allison French, though, they get a dollar."

The woman stood up and went back to the other girls in the back of the saloon. She was too fat to flounce, but she was trying.

"Think she gets many dollars?" I said to Virgil.

"Nope."

"Easy to turn down," I said.

Virgil shrugged.

"She probably don't like it, either," he said. "Just doing what she gotta."

A group of four men came into Los Lobos and stood at the bar and looked at Virgil. Each of them had a whiskey. Pretty soon two more men drifted in, and then three, until the bar was crowded with men.

"Looks like that kid been spreading the alert," I said to Virgil.

" 'Fraid so," Virgil said.

"All of 'em look like town people," I said. "Don't see no cowboys."

"Nope," Virgil said.

"I'm feeling a little left out," I said. "Nobody's looking at me."

"That's 'cause you're ugly," Virgil said.

"Wait a minute," I said. "Señorita offered me round the world for a dollar."

"She included you second," Virgil said.

"That's just 'cause I ain't famous like you," I said.

"Also true," Virgil said, and drank the last of his beer.

2

"I got enough change," I said, "I can buy two more beers. Save the dollar for a room."

"Maybe sleep in the livery stable," Virgil said. "I've slept in worse than a hayloft."

"We been sleeping in worse for most of the last year," I said.

Virgil nodded. He was looking at the bartender coming toward our table carrying a bottle and three glasses. With him was a short, wiry man. Not thin, exactly, but lean, sort of hard-looking, with a scraggly blond beard.

"You're Virgil Cole," the wiry man said as he reached the table.

Virgil nodded.

"Like to buy you a drink, if I can," the wiry man said.

"Sure can," I said, real quick, before Virgil could be unfriendly. You never knew with Virgil.

I gestured at an empty chair, and the wiry

man sat down. The bartender put three glasses on the table and poured a useful amount of whiskey in each one.

"Name's Cates," the wiry man said. "Everybody calls me Cates."

Virgil nodded and sipped his whiskey.

"Whiskey clears the throat," Virgil said. "Considerable better than beer."

"It does," Cates said. "You boys been traveling?"

Virgil nodded.

"This here's Everett Hitch," he said.

"By God," Cates said. "I heard a you, too."

"See that," I said to Virgil.

"You been with Mr. Cole for some time," Cates said.

"I have," I said.

Virgil grinned.

"Well," Cates said. "I'm proud to meet both you boys. Especially you, Mr. Cole."

" 'Specially," Virgil murmured to me.

"The great Virgil Cole," Cates said happily, "right here, in my saloon."

Virgil looked at me without expression.

"With his friend," Virgil said.

"Of course," Cates said. "With his friend, Mr. Hitch."

"Everett," I said. "And he won't mind you call him Virgil."

Virgil nodded. Cates nodded. And we all

drank. Cates picked up the bottle and poured us all some more. Cates looked around the room.

"Look at the crowd," he said. "Got to say you're a big attraction, Virgil."

"Like a geek show," Virgil said.

"No," Cates said. "God, no. It's respect. It's like a hero has come to town."

Virgil looked at me.

"Hero," he said.

"That'd be you," I said.

"Maybe you boys don't take it serious, but I'm here to tell you that we do."

" 'We'?" Virgil said.

"Everybody," Cates said. "I got a proposal for you."

Virgil didn't say anything. If Cates minded that, it didn't show.

"My shotgun lookout works 'bout twelve hours a day," Cates said. "He needs a break."

"Any law in town?" Virgil said.

"Never needed none," Cates said.

Virgil nodded.

"Like to hire you to sit shotgun," Cates said. "Couple hours a day is all, start of the evenin'."

"Draw a crowd?" I said.

"Sure would," Cates said. "The great Virgil Cole? Sitting shotgun in Los Lobos?

15

Good gracious. It would put this whole damned town on the map."

"And make you some money," I said.

"Sure would; why I want to do it. But what's good for me is good for the town, and the other way around as well."

"How much," Virgil said.

"Give you a dollar a day," Cates said.

"Each," Virgil said.

"You and Everett?" Cates said.

"Uh-huh."

Cates looked at the bar, which was two deep now with people drinking and watching Virgil. He looked at me and back at Virgil. Then he nodded.

"Done," he said.

He went into his pocket and took out two silver dollars and put them on the table.

"First day in advance," he said.

Virgil picked up the coins and gave one to me.

"Don't know how long I'll be in town," he said.

"Long as you're here, the deal stands," Cates said.

"I'm looking for a woman," Virgil said.

Cates grinned and waved his hand toward the back of the saloon.

"Take your pick," he said.

"Woman named Allison French," Virgil said.

"Can't say I know her," Cates said.

"Sings," Virgil said. "Plays the piano."

"In saloons?" Cates said.

"Yep."

"Lotta saloons in town," Cates said. "I can ask around."

"Do," Cole said.

3

We took a room in the Grande Palace Hotel, which was not accurately named, and agreed to live on Virgil's dollar a day and save mine for when we moved on. During Virgil's shift on lookout, I sat around Los Lobos and observed. During the day we strolled around the ugly little bare-board town and asked about Allie.

"When's the last time you did a lookout job?" I said to Virgil after the first night.

"Sorta helped you out a year ago up in Resolution," he said.

"But when did you actually earn money at it?" I said.

" 'Fore I met you," Virgil said.

"Close to twenty years," I said.

"Yep."

"How's it feel?" I said.

"People come here to look at me, Virgil Cole, the famous shooter. I feel like I'm in a circus."

"But . . ." I said.

"Need the money," he said.

"And we can't steal it," I said.

"Can't do that," Virgil said.

We were having breakfast in a cook tent that had no name, only a sign outside that said EAT. Virgil put down his coffee cup and looked at me.

"Ain't gonna talk about this 'cept once," Virgil said. "I got something I got to do. So I will do whatever I have to do to do it."

"Lotta do's in there, Virgil."

"You know what I'm saying."

I grinned at him.

"I do," I said.

"And you're with me."

"I am," I said.

"Because that's how we are," Virgil said.

I nodded.

"It is," I said.

"So I'm gonna sit lookout until we know that Allie ain't here. Then we gonna move on."

"I know," I said.

Virgil picked up his coffee cup and drank some.

"Coffee ain't very good," he said.

"Better than no coffee," I said.

Los Lobos was regularly jammed with

Virgil-watchers at the beginning of the evening. On the third night we were there, Cates came in and walked over to my table. I noticed that people made room for him quite carefully as he walked through the crowd. He seemed to be the most pleasant man in the room. But people were careful around him.

"Evenin', Everett," he said.

"Cates," I said.

"Mind if I sit with you?"

"Have a seat," I said.

Cates sat; the bartender brought him whiskey and two glasses. He poured himself a glass and offered some to me.

I shook my head.

"I'll drink a little beer," I said.

"Backing up Cole?" Cates said.

"Something like that."

"That why you got the shotgun?"

"Didn't know what else to do with it," I said. "Leave it someplace and somebody'll steal it."

Cates looked at the shotgun for a moment.

"That's some big load," he said.

"Eight-gauge," I said. "Brought it along with me when I left Wells Fargo."

"Blow a big hole," Cates said.

"Does," I said.

"Shotgun messenger?" Cates said.

"Yep."

"When'd you do that?"

"After I got out of the Army, I did a little of this, a little of that, 'fore I met Virgil."

"You enlisted?"

"Nope."

"West Point?" Cates said.

"Yep."

"I'll be damned," Cates said. "You never got along too well with the Army, I'm guessing."

"Lotta rules," I said. "How about you. How'd you end up here?"

"Come into a little money, sort of unofficial like," Cates said. "Bought this place when it was a rattrap. Hundreds of 'em. Got a couple big mean tomcats, fixed it up a little, and things are starting to build."

"Nothing like a tomcat," I said.

"Coyotes got one of 'em, but the other one's still working here," Cates said.

"Feed him?"

"Nope. He stays nice and fat on his own."

"Good thing," I said.

"Self-supporting," Cates said.

Cates poured himself a little more whiskey and looked at it in the glass. The room was thick with smoke, and noise, and the smell of whiskey.

"You still looking for that girl?" Cates said.

"Yep."

"Don't know if it's the right one, but there's a girl named Frenchie, works out of a saloon in the river end of town. Used to sing and play the piano some, they tell me. But she was pretty bad, so she mostly now just works on her back, if I can say that to you."

"You can," I said. "Won't do anybody any good to say it to Virgil, though."

There were some cards being played along the left wall of the saloon, and the whores clustered at the back, foraying out now and then for a prospect, taking him out through a door in the back of the room. They were generally not gone for long.

"No," Cates said. "I figured it wouldn't. Why I'm talking to you."

"What's the saloon?" I said.

"Barbary Coast Café," Cates said.

I smiled.

"Do get some names round here," Cates said. "Don't we."

"As grand as it sounds?" I said.

"No," Cates said.

We both looked at Virgil sitting motionless in the high chair, looking at nothing, seeing everything.

"Don't use a shotgun," Cates said.

22

"Mostly no," I said.

"Guess he don't need one," Cates said.

"Virgil don't need much," I said.

4

I left the eight-gauge with the bartender and went out into the darkening street. The dust was nearly ankle-deep on top of the hard-baked dirt beneath it. I walked toward the river. If I hadn't known where it was, I could have followed the smell of it. Around Los Lobos, among the saloons and bordellos, there were a few commercial enterprises that sold cloth and feed and nails. As I got closer to the river the shops disappeared and there were only saloons and whore-houses. The Barbary Coast Café was the last place on the street. It stood right up against the mudflat that bordered the de-pleted river. This time of year the Rio wasn't very grand. In spring the mudflats would be covered with water. But now there was mostly mud, with just enough water run-ning down the center to remind us it was a river.

The Barbary Coast was where it belonged.

It was a two-story building made of whatever they had available, some warped lumber that hadn't cured when they put it up
and was now warped and split from the dry-
ing process. Some of the roof was tin, some
was Mexican tile. Most of the windows had
no glass and were covered with something
that might have been flour sacks. The front
door, which stood open and looked like it
wouldn't close, appeared to have been
rendered from a wagon gate.

I went in. It was dark and smelled of coal
oil and smoke, full spittoons and sweat,
cigar smoke and booze. It wasn't crowded.
There were men lining the bar, which was
two planks on a couple of fifty-gallon kegs.
There were some cards being played by
candlelight at a few unmatched tables
around the room. Half the tables were
empty. And along the wall past the bar was
a small flock of desperate-looking whores.
The pickings looked slim. But repulsive. I
pulled my hat down over my eyes and went
to the bar, squeezed in among the other
men, for concealment, and ordered a beer.

"No beer," the barman said.

"Gimme what you got," I said.

The barman poured something from a jug
into a dirty glass. I sniffed it and put it
down.

"Frenchie around?" I said.

"Her?" the barman said.

"Her," I said.

The barman shrugged.

"Over there with the rest of 'em," he said. "Pink dress."

I looked at the whores. It was hard in the dim light, and I almost missed her. The pink dress was dirty. Her hair was ratty. She was a lot thinner than she had been, and the body that had once so proudly pushed at the confines of her dress now seemed shrunken inside her clothes. I studied her over the right shoulder of the fat man next to me. A lot less than she had been, but it was Allie. I watched her for a moment as she scanned the room, looking for prospects. Then I put a dime down beside my drink and moved away from the bar, not looking at Allie. The barman picked up my dime and then carefully poured the undrunk whiskey back into the jug.

I went back into the despondent street feeling tired and tight across my shoulders. So we'd found her. I didn't want Virgil to see her in this setting. But it wasn't for me to decide. It was the only setting she was in, and we'd spent a year looking for her. I started back up the street toward Los Lobos. For maybe the first time since I'd known Virgil, I didn't know what he would do.

5

Virgil didn't say a word from the time I told him we'd found Allie to the moment we stopped outside the rat hole where she worked. I had the eight-gauge with me, simply because I was more comfortable with it than without it, especially when I had no idea of what was going to happen.

Virgil studied the Barbary Coast Café.

"In there," he said.

"Yes."

Virgil looked at it some more. Then he nodded once and started forward, and we walked in through the front door. Virgil stopped inside to let his eyes adjust.

"Where is she?" Virgil said.

She was right where she had been. I nodded toward her. Virgil looked at her for a considerable time. Then he nodded again and walked over to her and stood in front of her. She looked up at him, forcing her customer's smile, started to speak, and stopped. The smile remained in place on her immobilized face. Virgil waited. She stared.

Then she said, "Virgil?"

Virgil nodded.

She said, "Virgil."

Virgil nodded.

She said, "Oh, sweet Jesus, Virgil, get me out of here."

"Yes," he said.

He took her arm and they started toward the door.

"Hey," the barman said. "Stairs in the back."

Virgil showed no sign that he'd heard.

"Whores ain't allowed to leave the premises," the barman said.

A fat man with a droopy mustache and long, greasy hair came from across the room and stood in the doorway.

"You planning on taking that whore somewhere?" he said.

There was a scar at one corner of his mouth, as if someone had cut him with a knife. He was wearing suspenders and no belt, and he had a Colt stuck in the right-hand pocket of his pants. With fluid economy, Virgil pulled his gun and slammed it against the fat man's head. The fat man went down. Virgil guided Allie around him

29

and out the front door.

The bartender said, "Hey."

I looked at him and shook my head. Then, with the eight-gauge leveled at the room, I backed out the front door and started up the street behind Virgil and Allie, keeping an eye over my shoulder at the Barbary Coast Café. Nobody came out.

Off the lobby of the Grande Palace Hotel there was a one-chair barbershop, and in the back of it was a small room, run by two fat old Mexican women, where you could get a bath. Virgil took Allie in there.

"Scrub her," he said to the two women. "And wash her clothes."

Allie stood motionless and silent.

"What she wear after?" one of the women said.

"We'll worry about that," Virgil said, "when she's clean."

6

Allie looked like a kid. Her hair was clean and straight. She wore no makeup, and she sat barefoot and cross-legged on the bed, wearing one of my clean shirts, like a dress, with the sleeves rolled.

"I could step out for a while," I said. "Get me a drink. Let you folks talk."

Virgil shook his head. So I sat on a chair in the corner of the room and was quiet.

"You run off," Virgil said to Allie.

"I was ashamed," she said.

"You sick at all?"

"No, honest to God, Virgil," she said. "I haven't got nothing."

"All this time you been whoring?" Virgil said.

"I know, but I been lucky. I haven't caught nothing."

Virgil nodded.

"You been whoring since you left."

Allie nodded slowly.

"Mostly," she said. "I had to live, Virgil."

Virgil nodded.

"You did," he said.

There was nothing in Virgil's voice. The single oil lamp next to the bed lit Allie pretty good, but it left most of the room sorta dark. The silence that hung between them seemed heavy.

"I was ashamed," Allie said. "And after Everett shot Bragg, I was scared."

"Of what?" Virgil asked.

"You," she said. "That you'd find out about me. Me, maybe, maybe I was scared of what I was."

"What were you?" Virgil said.

"I was an awful woman, I wanted everything, and being a woman, alone, out here in this country with no rules . . ."

"I had rules," Virgil said.

"And I was breaking them, Virgil. Only way I knew to get what I wanted, feel like I wanted to feel, be how I wanted, only way for me was to fuck somebody."

"Fucked a considerable number of somebodys," Virgil said.

"Yes," Allie said.

It was a child's voice, piping out from the fresh-scrubbed child's face. Virgil was silent. His face was in shadow. I was nearly invisible sitting away from the light in the corner.

"I shoulda stayed with you, Virgil."

"Yes," Virgil said. "You should have."

"But I was bad, just bad, all I can say. I run off and I tried but I could never find a decent man, never nobody like you, Virgil. And they passed me around and I kept going down, down, and down, and . . ." She stopped talking and took in a deep breath, and let it out very slow. She did it again.

Then she said, "I had to do some awful things, Virgil . . . awful things with awful men."

Virgil was silent. Allie looked down at her hands folded in her lap.

"Awful," she said.

Virgil stood suddenly and walked to the window and looked down through the darkness at the ugly street.

"And now?" he said.

"I guess I'm awful," she said. "I look awful. I feel awful. I ain't worth no man's attention. I ain't worth anything."

"You changed any?" Virgil said.

"I don't know," Allie said. "I'm at the bottom, Virgil. I can't go down no further."

"Think you could change?"

"I'd like to. I can't stand this no more. I'd surely try."

"What you think we should do?" Virgil said.

33

He was still looking down into the street.

"I don't know," Allie said in a really small voice. "I might just die."

Virgil didn't move from the window.

Still looking down into the street, he said, "Sooner or later. Everett, you got a thought?"

"I don't, Virgil. I don't believe it's mine to think about."

"You believe her?" Virgil said.

"I believe what's happened to her," I said.

"Think she can change?" Virgil said.

"Believe she wants to," I said.

"Think she can?"

"Don't know, Virgil."

Virgil turned slowly from the window and looked at me in the near darkness.

"Everett," Virgil said. "You killed a man for her and me. I want to know where you stand."

"You know where I stand, Virgil," I said. "Been with you near twenty years. Plan to be with you as far as we go."

"Think I should take her back?" Virgil said.

"Don't recall that she asked you to," I said.

"You think I should?" Virgil said. "I need to know what you think."

"We don't have to leave her here," I said. "We can take her someplace where she gets a decent chance."

"But you don't think I should take her back."

"She is what she is," I said. "Been what she is for a long time."

"And you don't think she'll change," Virgil said.

"Don't think she's got anything to change to," I said.

"You don't think I should take her back," Virgil said.

"No," I said. "I don't."

Allie's breathing was shallow in the silence. She seemed like an injured sparrow, sitting cross-legged on the bed in a shirt much too big for her, staring at her hands.

"No," Virgil said. His voice sounded hoarse. "I don't think so, either . . . but I got to do it."

I stood.

"It's yours to say," I told Virgil. "I'm going to bunk in the livery stable tonight."

Neither Virgil nor Allie said anything. Neither one moved as I left the room and closed the door behind me.

7

We took Allie to breakfast in the cook tent. With her dress washed and her hair combed, she looked a little better than she had when we dragged her out of the Barbary Coast Café. But she didn't look good.

"I got to get some new clothes, Virgil," she said.

"Next town," Virgil said.

"We leavin' this one?"

"Yep," Virgil said. "Can't make a livin' here."

"Virgil," Allie said, "I don't even have any underwear."

"Next town," Virgil said.

His eyes moved slightly and stopped. Then moved again. I was used to Virgil looking at things. If it was worth mentioning, he'd mention it.

"We need money," he said.

"Sell the horses?"

"Yes, livery stable will probably buy them.

Take what you can get; I don't want to wait around here."

"Saddles? bridles?"

"All of it," Virgil said. "And don't waste time. Want to catch today's train."

Virgil had seen something.

"On my way," I said.

Man doesn't sell his horse if he don't have to. The liveryman knew he had me in a box and got the horses and gear for a lot less than they were worth. Still, it would cover us for a bit. With the money in my pocket, I walked back up past the cook tent. Virgil and Allie weren't there. I went on to the hotel. When I got there they were packed, my stuff and Virgil's. Allie didn't have any. There wasn't much. Just the clothes would fit in a saddlebag. Virgil didn't run, so it must have to do with Allie. It was one of the many things I didn't like about Allie. I was used to Virgil being Virgil. He was always Virgil. But with Allie he was different. I didn't like different.

We went downstairs and walked to Los Lobos, where Virgil gave notice and shook hands with Cates. Then we went back out to the street and started toward the railroad station. Across the street a group of men watched us come out. And, when we started down the street they walked along with us on the other side. One of them was the fat man with the scar and the long hair that Virgil had buffaloed when we'd taken Allie out of the Barbary Coast Café.

Virgil paid them no mind as we walked.

"I count six," Virgil said to me softly. "Anything develops, I'll take the first man. You take the last, and we'll work our way to the middle."

I nodded. At this range, with the eight-gauge, I might get two at a time.

"Virgil," Allie said. "What is it."

"Nothing to worry about," Virgil said.

Allie looked for the first time at the men across the street.

"Oh my God, Virgil, it's Pig."

"That his name?" Virgil said.

"Don't let him take me back."

"Nope," Virgil said.

"Everett . . ."

"We're fine, Allie," I said. "We're fine."

Pig was carrying a big old Navy Colt in a gun belt that sagged under his belly. There was dried blood on his shirt. It appeared that he hadn't changed it since Virgil hit him. The left side of Pig's face was swollen and dark, with a long scab where Virgil's front sight had dragged across the cheek-bone. The five men with him were all carrying. I thumbed back both hammers on the eight-gauge.

We kept walking our parallel walk. Allie held tight to Virgil's left arm. At the end of the street was the Barbary Coast Café, and across the street from that the railroad station, and beyond that the river. And nothing else. It was obvious where we were going.

"I need you to let go of my arm now, Allie," Virgil said.

His voice was quiet. He could have been asking her to pass him the sugar. He was Virgil Cole again. Even with the stakes as high as they would ever get for him, he was now Virgil Cole. It was a relief. At the end of the street we stopped and the six men stopped across from us. The railroad station was on their side. We looked at one another. Pig was at the far left end of the line that now faced us.

"Hey, Whoreman," Pig shouted. "Whatcha gonna do now?"

"Same deal," Virgil said to me. "Pig goes first. You start at the right end."

"Yep."

"Allie," Virgil said. "Any shooting, you lie flat down in the street, you unnerstand?"

"Virgil . . ."

"Unnerstand?" Virgil said again.

His voice was still calm, but it had flattened a little.

"Yes," Allie said in a small voice.

"Okay," Virgil said, and stepped off the boardwalk and into the street.

Allie moved behind me. She was mumbling softly to herself, and after a moment I realized she was praying. Virgil walked straight across the street toward the six men, and specifically toward Pig.

I knew what he was doing. Never let it be you and them, Virgil always said. Always make it between you and some of them.

"I want my whore back," Pig said.

Virgil kept walking. Pig hadn't expected it. He wasn't quite sure what he should do.

"You think you gonna hit me again when I ain't ready?" Pig said.

"I'm gonna kill you," Virgil said.

Virgil didn't speak very loudly, but all of us heard him, and his voice made Pig flinch back a half step. I brought the eight-gauge up to a kind of parade rest position. The men to Pig's left moved a little away. Virgil was close now. If Pig was going to make his move he'd need to do it now, before Virgil was on top of him. He knew it, and tried to draw his gun. Virgil shot him before Pig got his hand on the butt. Without any pause Virgil shot the man next to him. I picked off the two at the other end of the line. The remaining two didn't know whether to shoot at me or Virgil and ended up running away.

Time slows down in a gunfight. Even so, including Virgil's walk across the street it had lasted less than a minute. Virgil reloaded and went to each of the down men to be sure they were dead. Then he holstered his gun and walked back.

"Train comes at noon," Virgil said.

And we walked on to the station.

8

We sat in the back of the train, on the left side, Virgil on the aisle. Virgil always sat on the left on the aisle so that his gun hand was unencumbered. Allie sat next to him. I sat across from them, facing the rear. Since people could board from either end, it was nice to watch both doors. The train bumped along. Virgil had his feet up and his hat tipped down. Allie sat erect beside him with her hands folded in her lap, looking out the window at the west Texas countryside. Occasionally, we passed cattle. Otherwise, there was nothing much to see but grassland.

"You ever pray, Everett?" Allie said.

"Not much," I said.

"Ever think about it?"

"Praying?"

"God," Allie said.

"Not much," I said.

"You know, after I run off," Allie said, "got

taken up by a Mexican man, I think. He took me a ways and sold me to couple men who were half Comanche. They kept me awhile and sold me to Pig."

I nodded. Virgil appeared to be asleep, though I doubted that he was.

"When I was in that place," Allie said, "I started praying. I prayed that Virgil would come and find me. And you too, Everett."

Allie didn't want to hurt my feelings.

"Heard you praying back in the street," I said.

"I was," Allie said. "I believe it helped."

"Didn't hurt," I said.

She nodded and went back to looking out the window. Virgil never stirred. The conductor came into our car, and the loud rattle of the train came in with him as he opened the door and passed from the next car to ours. When he came to us I handed him three tickets. He punched them and looked at the eight-gauge leaning against the corner of the seat by the window.

"What the hell's that thing?" he said.

"Eight-gauge shotgun," I said.

"You planning on hunting locomotives?" the conductor said.

"Only if one attacks me," I said.

"Be a fool if it did," he said, looking at the eight-gauge. "Where you folks headed."

43

"Next town, I guess," I said.

"That'd be Greavy," he said. "You got business in Greavy."

"Looking for work," I said.

The conductor looked at Virgil and at me and at the eight-gauge. From the corner of his eye, he took a quick look at Allie in her pathetic dress and ratty Mexican sandals. But he didn't look long.

"I guess you're not cowboys," he said.

"No," I said. "We ain't."

"Well, good luck with it," the conductor said.

"How long to Greavy?" I said.

"Maybe another hour or so," the conductor said.

"Got a place there to buy ladies' clothes?" I said.

"Sure, up-and-coming little town, Greavy. Got a good general store. Sells most everything."

"Thanks," I said.

He gave his cap bill a little tug and headed back down the train.

Nobody said anything for a while. Virgil remained motionless.

Then Allie turned from the window and said, "Thank you for asking about the clothes, Everett."

I was pretty sure that was for Virgil. I was

44

pretty sure all of her conversation had been for Virgil. She knew he wasn't sleeping.

"Pleasure," I said.

9

Greavy was an improvement over Placido. It was neat. Several of the buildings were painted. There were two restaurants, a bank, a big general store, and a big livery stable. We got Allie some clothes, ate some boiled beef and pinto beans at Chez Barcelona, and strolled on down to the marshal's office. Allie hung back as we went in, and stood outside near the door. The marshal was a square-built man named Sheehan. He was as tall as Virgil and a little shorter than me. He wasn't wearing a gun, though a Winchester lay on the desk beside him as we talked.

"Nope, sorry, boys," he said. "Got six deputies already. More than the town needs except when they bring cattle in. You boys been marshaling before?"

"We have," Virgil said.

"Whereabouts?" Sheehan said.

"All over," Virgil said. "Most recent, I

guess, we was in Appaloosa."

"Appaloosa?" Sheehan said. "How recent?"

"Couple years now, ain't it, Everett?"

" 'Bout," I said.

"You ain't Virgil Cole?" Sheehan said.

"I am," Virgil said.

"Jesus Christ," Sheehan said.

"Wasn't you up in Resolution last year?"

"I was, but I weren't marshaling," Virgil said. "This here's Everett Hitch."

"Sure thing," Sheehan said. "I know who you are. You boys are famous."

"Know any gun work around here?" I said.

"Maybe," Sheehan said. "I don't think he's pressed, but the railroad just expanded service to Brimstone, up north a ways. They're building new stock pens, more cattle coming in. And Dave Morrissey was saying last time I saw him he might need to add a couple gun hands."

"Who's Morrissey?" Virgil said.

"Val Verde County sheriff," Sheehan said. "Up there filling in right now, 'cause he had a deputy quit on him."

"Why'd the deputy quit?" Virgil said.

"Got married; wife insisted it was too dangerous."

"How far up north," Virgil said.

" 'Bout two days' ride," Sheehan said.

"Virgil Cole! By God! What I'm gonna do is I'm gonna wire Dave, tell him you're coming. Tell him not to hire no one else."

" 'Preciate it," Virgil said.

Allie came into the office almost tiptoe-ing.

" 'Scuse me, Marshal," she said. "I'm Allie French. I'm with these gentlemen, and I just bought some clothes. Do you suppose I could go into one of your cells and change?"

"Cells?"

"Long as you promise not to peek," she said.

Sheehan looked at Virgil. Virgil nodded faintly.

"Sure thing, ma'am," Sheehan said. He opened the door to the cell row.

"We got no guests at the moment," he said. "Use any cell."

Sheehan looked at us for a moment and decided not to ask anything.

"Whyn't you boys wait here for the lady," Sheehan said. "And I'll go over and send Dave a telegram. Time you get there, he'll be waiting for you."

10

We bought a buckboard and a mule for about what we'd sold one of the horses for. And with me driving, and Allie between us on the seat, we set out the next morning for Brimstone. Allie's new clothes were an improvement. She had a ribbon in her hair. And she was wearing a little makeup. She was still kind of skinny. But she was looking better.

We were quiet. The buckboard was easy enough through the low grasslands, for a buckboard. There's a reason it's called a buckboard, and an easy ride ain't it. The mule plodded along a sort of wagon rut west toward the Paiute River. It was sunny and hot. We could hear the soft coo of doves, and occasionally we kicked up a flutter of them as we rode by. We passed cattle. Mostly shorthorns, but still now and then a longhorn bull.

Virgil was looking at the landscape.

"Wolves," he said.

The mule must have caught scent of them. He tossed his head and shied and made a short snorting sound. I didn't see them yet. Then I did, three gray shapes trotting in line, heading east, appearing and disappearing in the high grass.

"Following that cattle herd," I said.

"Likely," Virgil said.

"Are you going to shoot them?" Allie said.

"No reason," Virgil said.

"But the cattle . . ." Allie said.

"Not my cattle," Virgil said.

"But the poor cows," Allie said.

"What you think them cows are for, Allie? Wolves eat 'em. People eat 'em. Don't seem to me make much difference to the cow."

Allie watched them until they were gone, and the mule settled back into his walk.

"How'd you see them so quick, Virgil," Allie said.

"Eyesight's good," he said.

"But it's more than that, isn't it?" Allie said. "You always see everything."

Virgil didn't answer. We rode in silence for a while.

Then Allie said, "You know what I'd like to do again?"

Virgil didn't say anything.

So I said, "What's that, Allie."

"I'd like to be Allie again."

"Be nice," I said.

"It would," Allie said.

Virgil was looking at the landscape again.

"Virgil isn't very talkative," Allie said. "Is he, Everett."

"Don't seem so," I said.

"Used to be a talker," Allie said.

I nodded.

"How come you don't talk to us, Virgil?" Allie said.

"Got nothing to say," Virgil answered.

"When we were together in Appaloosa," Allie said, "you used to talk a lot about nothing."

"Lotta things happened since Appaloosa," Virgil said.

"You thinking about all those things, Virgil?" Allie said.

"Yep."

"Wasn't easy on me, you know?" Allie said.

"I know."

"You gonna stop thinking about all that, one of these days?" Allie said.

"Might," Virgil said.

Nobody said anything else. I looked over at Allie once and saw that her lips were moving. Appeared she was praying again. Other than that, we bumped along in silence until we reached the Paiute River, where we

51

made camp and slept under the buckboard.

11

We headed north along the Paiute at sunrise, and by the middle of the afternoon we were in a hotel in Brimstone, Allie and Virgil in one room, me next door.

"Heard you was out of the law business," Dave Morrissey said when we went to see him.

"Was," Virgil said.

"What changed your mind?" Morrissey said.

Virgil was silent for a moment.

"Well, some things bothered me," Virgil said. "But Everett and I talked some, and now they don't bother me so much."

I was startled. First time he'd ever admitted that I had any influence on him.

"Anything else?" Morrissey said.

Virgil grinned.

"Need the money," he said.

Morrissey nodded.

"Ain't quite commensurate with the risk,"

he said. "But only a fool would do it for free."

"How 'bout you, Hitch?" Morrissey said.

He looked like he might have been a cowboy once, sort of bowlegged and smallish. He had a big drooping mustache, and wore a long duster.

"Well," I said, "I done law and not law for a long time. Don't make a lot of difference to me. I'm not too scared, and I'm decent with the eight-gauge."

"That's what that thing is," Morrissey said. "Thought it might be a cannon."

"Two barrels," I said.

Morrissey grinned.

"God's truth," he said. "I heard about you boys, and when Sheehan telegrammed me I was interested. I'm told you'll stand, and your word is good."

"It is," Virgil said.

"And I hire you, you won't sell me out for a higher offer."

"We don't promise to work for you forever," Virgil said. "But we won't work against you, 'less you force it."

"Fair enough," Morrissey said. "What I told Sheehan was true, we're booming. Cattle mostly. Railroad's expanding, bigger herds coming in. I come down from Del Rio every once in a while, and a Ranger comes by every month or so. But right now there ain't no permanent law here, and the place is growing like a damn weed."

"Town grows too fast," Virgil said, "leaves an empty space; people fight to fill it."

"You've worked a lot of towns," Morrissey said.

"We have," Virgil said.

"The situation in this one is a little peculiar," Morrissey said. "We have a fella named Pike. I don't even know his first name. Everyone calls him Pike. . . . Hell, maybe Pike is his first name."

Virgil shrugged.

"Anyway," Morrissey said, "he showed up here a few years ago with the remains of a gang that the Pinkertons chased into exhaustion."

"They'll do that," I said.

"Sometimes," Morrissey said. "He had a few of his boys with him and some money they probably stole from a railroad, and they bought a saloon at the north end of town. Never broke no law here. And they run a first-class operation. Booze is good, games are honest, girls are clean. They police themselves. No trouble. We've never even had to go up there since they been in town."

"Model citizens," I said.

"And then, 'bout a year ago, here come

Brother Percival."

"Percival," Virgil murmured.

"What he calls himself," Morrissey said. "Brother Percival."

"Preacher?" I said.

"Yep," Morrissey said. "Come to town with a tent show, preaching against sin like he was the first man to discover it. Nobody paid him much attention for a time. But he kept collecting people to his whatever it is, and then he built himself a church, brought in a damned organ from Kansas City. And him and some of the people come with him when he arrived, they decide to make a target of the biggest and best saloon in town."

"Pike's," Virgil said.

"What's Brother Percival want?" I said.

"Damned if I know. Maybe he is acting on behalf of the Kingdom of Heaven. Maybe he wants to take over Texas."

"And Pike?" I said.

Morrissey smiled a little.

"He wants to take over Texas," Morrissey said.

"Potential there for conflict," Virgil said.

Morrissey nodded.

"You want the job?" he said.

"Sure," Virgil said.

12

"Commensurate?" Virgil said outside Morrissey's office.

"Sort of like equal to," I said.

"Might as well go right at 'em," Virgil said. "See what we got."

"Which one first?" I said.

"Start with Pike," Virgil said.

"More our type," I said.

"Ain't so sure we got a type," Virgil said.

Brimstone was about seven blocks wide and ten blocks long in a green bend of the Paiute River, which made it cooler than this part of Texas usually was. Pike's Palace was halfway down Arrow Street, on the west corner of Fifth Street, putting it about in the center of the town. All around it, the town was busting out of its skin. Freight and lumber were being hauled through town. Buildings were going up, saloons and eating places were crowded, and there were two general stores, a bowling alley, two millinery shops, and two hotels already and a third one being built. The air was full of sounds: wagons creaking, men swearing, mules, oxen, carpentry, and blacksmithing. At the north end of Arrow Street was a big town hall, almost finished. At the south end was a church with an imposing spire. There were boardwalks lining every street, and most of the buildings had roofed out over the boardwalk in front of them, so you could shelter from the sun in good weather and the rain in bad.

The saloon had a corner entrance and heavy oak doors, which were opened back in good weather and let you into a vestibule with swinging doors ornamented by stained-glass windows. Through the swinging doors was the saloon.

Wearing our new deputy stars, we stopped inside the doorway and looked around.

"Pike done himself proud," Virgil said.

"Did," I said.

Along the length of one wall, which seemed from inside to run nearly the whole block along Fifth Street, was an elaborate mahogany bar with a black mirrored wall behind it and bottles stacked in decorative pyramids. Along the other wall was a row of gaming tables, and in the open space between were tables and matching chairs.

There was an ornate chandelier shedding light on the windowless room, and at the back a set of stairs that led to a second floor. The wide plank floors were polished. The bar top gleamed. The saloon whores were neat. And the glassware appeared clean. Four bartenders worked the bar, which was busy in the late afternoon, and a thin, dark, sharp-faced guy with a shotgun sat in the lookout chair near the far end of it. Virgil walked down the length of the bar to him.

"J.D.," he said.

The lookout examined Virgil.

Then he said, "Wickenburg."

"Yep."

"Virgil Cole," J.D. said.

"Yep."

"You posted us out of town," J.D. said.

"You was with Basgall," Virgil said.

"Moved on," J.D. said.

"And Basgall?"

"Got shot by two Texas Rangers in El Paso."

"You with Pike now?" Virgil said.

"I work here," J.D. said. "You?"

"Me and Hitch here signed on with the sheriff," Virgil said.

"Seen the badges," J.D. said.

"Like to talk with Pike," Virgil said.

J.D. nodded.

"Spec," he said to one of the bartenders, "go tell Pike new deputy wants to see him."

"Name's Virgil Cole," Virgil said.

Spec nodded and walked to a door under the back stairs. In a moment he returned, and behind him was a big man with very little hair and a short beard.

"Virgil Cole," he said, and put his hand out.

Virgil didn't take it.

"This here's Everett Hitch," Virgil said.

Pike didn't seem to mind not shaking hands.

"Good to meet you, Everett," he said. "You fellas care for a drink?"

"Beer'd be good," Virgil said.

Pike nodded at the bartender and led us to an empty table.

"Bartender says you and J.D. know each other," Pike said.

"Wickenburg," Virgil said.

The bartender arrived with three mugs of beer and placed them carefully before us.

"Thank you, Spec," Pike said.

He raised his mug toward us. We drank.

"J.D. is a pretty good gun hand," Pike said.

"Was," Virgil said.

"Still is," Pike said.

"Likely so," Virgil said. "I just ain't seen him lately."

Pike was deceptive. When you first saw him you thought he was fat. But when he moved he seemed light on his feet, and quick. And when you sat with him, up close, and could look at him you realized that he was big and barrel-shaped, but not much of it was fat. I looked around the saloon.

"Done yourself proud here, Mr. Pike," I said.

"Aw, just Pike. Nobody calls me Mister."

"Well, you got a nice place here," I said.

"Yeah, lotta work, but it makes me sorta proud to see how it's come along," Pike said.

Virgil was quiet. I knew he was studying Pike.

"Understand you used to run a gang," I said.

"Yep, gotta say I did," Pike said. "Done some pretty illegal things for a while until the damn Pinkertons wore me out. Had all that railroad money behind them . . ." He shook his head.

"So you came here," I said.

"Yep, ain't broke a law in Texas," he said. "Had some money saved, brought a few of my boys, bought a damned shack of a place with no name, and we went to work."

"J.D. one of the boys you brought?" Virgil said.

"Yep, J.D. is a good man, and I believe in

loyalty."

Virgil nodded.

"Other lookout, Kirby Harris, was with me, too."

Pike nodded toward the bartender who'd brought us the beer.

"Spec," he said. "Few other boys."

"Whadda they do?" Virgil said.

"They help me with some of my other interests," Pike said. "I'm expanding."

"What else you do?" Virgil said.

"Oh, this and that," Pike said. "Lemme get you boys another beer."

He gestured at Spec. I noticed he'd drunk only a little of his.

Virgil didn't push his question.

"Any trouble in town?" Virgil said.

"Why do you ask?" Pike said.

"Just trying to get the lay of the land," Virgil said. "Who's that German guy you studied at West Point?"

"Clausewitz," I said.

"Yeah," Virgil said, "him."

He looked at Pike.

"Fella says you need to be prepared for what can happen, you know, not for what might."

Pike nodded.

"You went to West Point, Mr. Hitch?"

"Everett," I said. "And Virgil won't mind

62

if you call him Virgil."

Pike smiled and nodded.

"You go to the Academy, Everett?"

"I did."

"When?"

I told him.

"Why we didn't meet," Pike said. "I was there a little earlier."

"You in the Army?" I said.

"Yep. Soldiered for ten years. Out here mostly," Pike said.

"Indian wars?" I said.

Pike nodded.

"Southern Cheyenne. Apache, Kiowa, Comanche. Comanches were a bitch."

"Still are," I said.

"Got to be a captain," Pike said. "But . . ."

He shook his head.

"Rules got to be too much," he said.

"Yep," I said.

"You too?" Pike said.

I nodded.

"Yep."

"How you get along with Brother Percival?" Virgil said.

Pike looked as if he'd been brought back from a reverie.

"Brother Percival," he said, and shook his head. "Brother Percival."

"Understand he's opposed to sin," Virgil said.

"Appears so," Pike said. "Which can be identified by seeing if people enjoy it."

"And if they do?" Virgil said.

"It's sin," Pike said.

"You seem to be selling a lot of it here," Virgil said.

"Much as I can," Pike said.

"He bother you?" Virgil said.

"So far a lotta blah, blah," Pike said.

"You think there might be more?" Virgil said.

There was no meaning in his voice, just aimless talk. Except, if you knew Virgil, you knew there was nothing aimless about him.

"He's got a lot of hard-looking deacons," Pike said.

"What do you think that means?" Virgil said.

"Might just mean he needs a lot of people to make the collections," Pike said.

"Or?" Virgil said.

"Virgil," Pike said. "I gotta tell you, I don't know. I don't understand Brother Percival. I don't know if he's a God-fearing Christian, or a lunatic, or a rogue. He might be running a church or a flimflam. His deacons may be prayerful or they may be troops. What I know is I don't like him."

"And you have a few troops of your own," Virgil said.

Pike smiled.

"Some," he said.

"Left over from the old days."

"Some."

"Doing this and that," Virgil said.

"Exactly," Pike said.

"So you're prepared."

"Me and Mr. Clausewitz," Pike said.

He grinned at both of us.

"Plus," he said, "I know you boys'll protect me."

"Sure thing," Virgil said.

13

We ate dinner at the hotel with Allie, and then the three of us sat outside on the front porch of the hotel and watched the evening action on Arrow Street. Virgil and Allie sat on a bench. I had my own chair. A lot of towns Virgil and I had worked were whores and drunks, teamsters and drovers and thugs. Brimstone was an actual town. Women walked along the street, some with children. Men who might work in banks strolled along with them. In the street among the horses and wagons were neat carriages, one- and two-horse rigs, with leather seats and canvas canopies to keep the rain off.

"I found a house for rent," Allie said. "Other end of Seventh Street. They're building a whole row of them."

Virgil nodded.

"Got a kitchen, got a front room, bedroom, got a room for Everett," Allie said.

"Be cheaper than the hotel, and Everett could chip in."

"Sounds fine, Allie," Virgil said.

"I can cook for both of you. I can wash and iron your clothes, and clean up. Make you breakfast in the morning."

"That'd be nice, Allie," Virgil said.

"Can we do it?" Allie said. "I'll take care of everything."

"Sure," Virgil said.

"Oh, Virgil," Allie said, putting her arms around Virgil and pressing her face into his neck. Virgil didn't move.

Allie straightened up and patted her hair.

"We'll move in tomorrow," she said. "I'll do it. You want me to move your stuff, Everett."

"Ain't much to move," I said. "I'll take care of it when you tell me."

"Oh, this is grand," Allie said. "This will be grand."

Virgil nodded. The sun was down, the street was darkening, and the air was warm and still. There were no streetlamps yet, but a lot of the merchants hung lanterns outside their doorways, and the soft light made Arrow Street look serene as the night came down.

Allie was looking at the lights.

"I'm going to make it up to you, Virgil. To

both of you," Allie said. "You too, Everett. I've been awful to both of you."

She was including me to be polite, and I knew it.

"I want to change," she said. "I don't want to be that woman, that Allie, anymore. I want to be a good woman, take care of a man, sing in the church, keep a proper house."

Neither Virgil nor I spoke. Allie was staring at the lights, in some sort of dream, and I wasn't even sure she was talking to Virgil.

"I was in the bottom of the pit in Placido," she said. "The bottom, no way to go down deeper. I was gonna die there."

She looked at Virgil.

"And then you came, and you brought me out."

"Everett and me," Virgil said.

"Yes, Everett, too. And it was like you were from heaven come to save me, and you did; after all I done to drive you away, you found me and you saved me."

"I ain't one for giving up on things," Virgil said.

"And you bore me away and brought me here," Allie said.

"On a buckboard," Virgil said.

"Oh, don't tease me," Allie said. "This is too much. . . . I got too much feeling. I'm gonna change, Virgil, I swear to God, I swear. . . . I'm changing now, I can feel it going on."

"Good," Virgil said. "You was looking a bit peaked when I found you."

"That's not what I'm talking about, Virgil."

"I know it ain't, Allie," Virgil said.

They were both quiet. I was, too. I had my own views on Allie's potential for change, but sharing them didn't seem like a useful thing. So I stayed quiet.

"You ain't touched me since you found me in Placido," Allie said.

I concentrated hard on watching the people moving through the lantern light. I wasn't sure Allie even remembered I was there. But whether she did or not, this wasn't a conversation I wanted to join.

"Things take time," Virgil said.

"Like finding me," Allie said.

"Took a lotta time," Virgil said.

"But you're not one for giving up on things," Allie said.

"I am not," Virgil said.

"So maybe you'll find me again," Allie said.

"Expect I will," Virgil said.

14

The white clapboard building looked like a Congregational church in some town in Vermont. Except it was at the south end of Arrow Street in Brimstone, beside the Paiute River, in the middle of the Texas prairie. A sign over the door read *The Church of the Brotherhood.* Brother Percival was giving his morning service when Virgil and I came in. We took off our hats and stood at the rear of the church while Brother Percival told us in unpleasant detail what hell was like and how easy it was to get there.

He was a big, strapping man, with blond hair to his shoulders. His eyes were big and the sort of hard bright blue you see in Navajo jewelry. He was dressed in a white robe and sandals. His voice was deep and reached without apparent effort to every corner of the big church.

"There is a long and slippery slope," he

said, "that all of us live on. It is called this world, and there are no handholds. And all those who live only in this world begin slowly to slide, slowly, slowly, to slide toward the pit."

There was no religious ornamentation in the church. Merely a big crucifix on the wall behind Brother Percival, and a polished mahogany altar rail in front of him. As he preached he walked back and forth behind the rail.

"And the closer to the pit we get, the faster we slide, and we reach out, and we try to stop but there is nothing to stop us, this downsloping world has nothing to hang on to and we slide faster and faster, weighted down by all the things of this world, surely and ever more surely toward the pit."

The interior of the church was painted white. The windows on either side of the church were the same pale glinting blue as the preacher's eyes. Above us where we stood, in the back of the church, was a balcony. I couldn't see from where I stood, but I assumed the Kansas City organ was up there.

"God alone is our handhold, and his kingdom is not of this world. We grasp frantically, trying to hang on to the things of this world, all the while turning our backs to our only hope for rescue, for salvation, for escaping the raging inferno of the eternal pit."

The church was nearly full, men and women, maybe more women. Along the walls stood hatless men in black suits and white shirts.

"The main business of this community is whores and whiskey and gambling with cards. It is a community run by people who trade on human weakness, on lust, and thirst, and greed. It is a community of the godless."

The audience was entirely still, motionless in their church pews, listening to the word of the Lord. The men along both walls nodded their heads silently. The morning sun shining through the pale blue windows gave a blue tone to everything.

"But we are not godless," Brother Percival roared. "We are the godly, and we are growing, and as we grow, a new and ever more muscular love of righteousness will grow with us and spread through this community and drive out the pustulating corruption, and the Lord God Almighty will prevail here as He must everywhere, and we will prevail here in His name."

Brother Percival was sweating. His face was shiny with sweat. His muscular neck was glistening with sweat, and as he turned in his pacing behind the altar rail, the sweat was darkening the back of his white robe between his shoulder blades.

"We will prevail," he said softly.

He stood erect and spread his arms.

"We will prevail," he said louder.

"In God's name, and with his strength" — he was bellowing now — "we . . . will . . . prevail."

Then he stopped and stood for a moment with his arms spread wide and his face raised to the ceiling. The room was dead still. Then he dropped his arms and buried his face in his hands and stood exhausted. Then the room erupted. Men and women were clapping. Many were screaming, "We will, we will." Most rose to their feet. The clapping was sustained, and as it and the screaming went on, the men in the dark suits began to move down each of the aisles, passing collection baskets.

Virgil and I stayed where we were while the tempest and the collection ran their course, during which time Brother Percival stood motionless in the front of the church with his face in his hands.

I looked at Virgil.

"Fella knows an awful lot about hell," I said.

Virgil nodded and smiled at me. "So do we," he said.

15

When the collection was taken and the money stored, and the baskets put away, and the last of the churchgoers had left the church, the deacons went back to their positions along the walls. Only then did Brother Percival raise his face. He seemed to have collected himself during the interlude. He saw Virgil and me standing in the back and opened the altar-rail gate and walked down the center aisle of the church toward us. Up close, he was impressive. Bigger than I was, and muscular. He looked at us calmly for a moment.

Virgil introduced himself and me.

"New deputies," Percival said.

"We are," Virgil said.

"Here on the Lord's business?" Percival said.

"Sort of all the Lord's business, ain't it?" Virgil said.

"Suppose it is," Percival said. "But some

of it is Satan's business, too."

"Well, we're all opposed to that," Virgil said.

"I hope so," Percival said.

Virgil surveyed the church.

"Heard you had an organ," he said.

"In the choir loft," Percival said. "The Lord has yet to send us someone to play it."

Virgil nodded.

"I'm sure," Virgil said, "that he'll send someone soon."

"As am I," Percival said.

There was a quality of ironic artificiality in his bearing that was hard to figure. It was like we all knew he was a fraud and it amused him to pretend he wasn't. . . . Or maybe he wasn't a fraud.

"Lotta deacons," Virgil said.

"We are not lambs," Percival said. "Ours is a leonine Christianity."

Virgil looked at me.

"Leonine," he said, as if he were tasting the word.

"Like a lion," I said.

Virgil nodded.

"Leonine," he said again. "I like it."

He looked at the deacons some more, then he walked to the line up along the right-hand wall and stopped in front of the first deacon, and looked at him closely.

"Choctaw," Virgil said. "Choctaw Brown." The deacon looked at him impassively.

"Lemme think," Virgil said.

Nobody moved. The deacon remained impassive. He was about Virgil's size, and flat-faced.

"Lambert, New Mexico," Virgil said. "You was with Charlie Dyer's bunch."

"You must have Deacon Brown confused," Percival said, "with someone else."

"Pretty good gun hand," Virgil said, "as I recall."

"As I say, Brother Cole," Percival said, "you must have Deacon Brown confused with another."

Virgil nodded and walked back to Percival.

"So," Virgil said. "Your lee-o-nine business causing any trouble for you with folks in town?"

"None that we cannot handle," Percival said. "We are doing God's work."

Virgil smiled.

"I'm sure He's pleased about that," Virgil said.

"God exists in each of us," Percival said.

"Sure," Virgil said. "How you get along with the folks at Pike's Palace."

"Pike's is a stew of corruption," Percival said.

"Got a plan for that?" Virgil said.

"We are guided by the Lord," Percival said.

"Damn," Virgil said. "Makes me kind of envious, seeing as how me and Everett are mostly on our own."

"You are both welcome at services," Percival said.

"Thank you," Virgil said.

"Ours is a militant Christianity," Percival said.

"Me and Everett are kinda militant ourselves," Virgil said.

"But despite our militancy," Percival said, "we are brothers to every Christian person."

Virgil looked at me.

"We like that, Everett?" he said.

"Not always," I said.

And we left.

16

We walked back to the sheriff's office past the railroad station. Six new cattle pens were nearly finished, and there was enough lumber stacked to suggest that there'd be more.

"Be a lot of drovers," I said. "All loose and looking for trouble."

Virgil grinned at me.

"Wait'll they get a look at us," he said.

I nodded.

"Wait'll," I said.

Morrissey had gone back to Del Rio. And the sheriff's office was ours. There was a cell block behind the office, with four cells, none of them at the moment occupied. There was a desk, at which Virgil sat, and a couple of straight chairs, and an odd-looking bow-backed couch with some faded red pillows on it against the left wall. I sat on the couch.

"Choctaw Brown," I said.

"Yep," Virgil said. "Quick, likes shooting. I killed his partner back in Lambert, a long time ago. 'Fore I met you."

"J.D.," I said.

"J.D. Sisko," Virgil said. "He can shoot."

"So they both got one," I said.

"One?" Virgil said. "They both got about twenty, way I see it."

"You don't think the deacons are godly?" I said.

" 'Bout as godly as you," Virgil said.

"How you know I ain't godly," I said.

"Are you?"

"No," I said.

"That's how I know," Virgil said. "I happen to know one of the shooters on each side. I'm betting they ain't the only ones."

"Probably not," I said.

Allie came into the office carrying an iron pot of something. She looked well-scrubbed and neat. There was some color in her cheeks now, and she seemed to have put on a few pounds.

"Brought you boys some lunch," Allie said. "Just made it this morning."

She put the pot on the desk, went to a cupboard on the right wall, took out a couple of tin plates and two spoons, and set them out beside the pot on Virgil's desk.

"Can't stay and eat with you," she said. "I

80

got some errands to run. I'll come back in a while, though, and clean up."

"Thank you," Virgil said.

"That's very kind of you, Allie," I said. "No need to come back, though. We can clean up."

"No," she said. "Won't hear of it. You got your job and I got mine. I'll be back in an hour or so."

She smiled, blew us both a kiss, and went.

Virgil and I sampled the stew. It was bad. Virgil made a face as he swallowed.

"Jesus," he said.

I tried a small sample.

"I see what you mean," I said.

"You want any more?" he said.

"No," I said.

Virgil picked up the pot and went to the door and looked out. Allie was not in sight. He went out and around to the back of the cell block and dumped the stew, and came back in with the empty pot.

"You gonna tell her we ate it all?" I said.

"Sure," Virgil said.

"Won't that encourage her to make more?" I said.

"I suppose," Virgil said. "But at least we'll know what to expect."

I nodded.

"Otherwise, she might try something

81

else," I said.

"She ain't gonna quit," Virgil said.

"At least she's trying," I said.

"Might be better if she weren't," Virgil said. "She's been washing and ironing my shirts. Now half of them got a burn mark, where she gets the iron too hot or leaves it in the same place too long."

"She'll learn," I said.

"Maybe. Maybe I don't even want her to. Maybe I liked her better when she was singing in saloons."

"Except when you didn't," I said.

"Don't need to be delicate with me, Everett," Virgil said. "I didn't like it when she was fucking the patrons."

"Most folks wouldn't," I said.

"Why you suppose she was like that?" Virgil said.

I shook my head.

"Don't know," I said. "I'd guess she was scared. Been on her own most of her life, and the only way she had to . . . you know . . . get anything . . . get anyone to do anything was to pull up her skirt."

"I suppose," Virgil said. "But when she was with me?"

I shrugged.

"She was with you," I said.

"And when I wasn't around?" Virgil said.

"She was with somebody else. Somebody to take care of her."

"Like Ring Shelton," he said.

"Like Ring," I said.

"Would you stay with her?" Virgil said.

"No," I said. "Probably wouldn't."

"I ain't touched her since I got her back," Virgil said.

"Not ready?" I said.

"Not yet," he said.

"Why do you hang on to her?" I said.

"Don't know," Virgil said.

"Never seen you," I said, "not know what you needed to know."

"Except Allie," he said.

"Must be scaring hell out of her," I said. "Not having any sex with you."

"She got hold of a Bible someplace," Virgil said. "Been reading it a lot."

"Anything that keeps her from cooking," I said.

Virgil nodded.

"Lemme ask you something about the Bible," he said.

"Don't know much about the Bible," I said. "Never got much past the 'begets' stuff."

Virgil nodded.

"Adam and Eve were the first humans, right?" he said.

"I guess."

"And they had two sons, Cain and Abel, right?"

"I guess," I said again.

"And all the rest of us descended from them."

"Far as I know," I said.

"So who'd Cain and Abel mate with?"

"Check with Allie on that," I said.

Virgil grinned.

"Or Br'er Percival," he said.

"Even better," I said. "Want to go get something to eat 'fore Allie comes back and catches us?"

"Be fools not to," Virgil said.

17

A short, thick man with a big hat and a two-day growth of beard came into the sheriff's office.

"Which of you boys is the sheriff," he said.

"Both deputies," Virgil said. "Sheriff's in Del Rio."

"Name's Lester," he said. "Abe Lester. I'm trail boss for an outfit with quite some number of cows milling around at the moment about a day outside of town."

Virgil nodded.

"Virgil Cole," he said. "This here's Everett Hitch."

"Pleased," Lester said. "We'll bring 'em in tomorrow, and I just wanted to give you boys a little notice."

"How many cows?" Virgil said.

" 'Bout four thousand," Lester said. "Won't know exact till we tally."

"How many drovers?"

"Forty-eight," Lester said. "Plus one

wrangler, the cook, and me."

"Can you control 'em?" Virgil said.

Lester smiled.

"Cattle? Sure," Lester said.

"How 'bout the cowboys?" Virgil said.

"They'll drive the cattle into town tomorrow and herd 'em into the pens," Lester said. "That's what they signed on for. When they're done I pay 'em off."

"You control them until you pay 'em?"

"Always have," Lester said.

"And after?"

"Ain't mine anymore," Lester said.

"Guess they get to be mine," Virgil said. "And Everett's."

"I'd say so," Lester said.

"Why they pay us," Virgil said.

"You the same Virgil Cole was in Abilene a while back?" Lester said.

"I was in Abilene."

"So I guess you know how," Lester said.

"We do," Virgil said.

Lester looked at me and nodded.

"One other thing, I guess you should know," Lester said. "Two, two and a half days ago, we run into a few Indians."

"Comanche?"

"Probably," Lester said. "They slaughtered a couple of cows."

"You see 'em?"

"Nope."

"How you know it was Indians."

"One of the drovers is a breed," Lester said. "Can read sign. Says the horses weren't shod. Actually, said it might be only one horse."

Virgil nodded.

"So it might be only one Indian," he said.

"Maybe. Either way. Somebody left an arrow stuck into one of the dead steers," Lester said. "Like some kind of sign."

"Your breed know what?" Virgil said.

"Garr don't know. Says it looks like a Comanche arrow, but he don't know why it's there."

"Didn't kill the steer with it?" Virgil said.

"Nope. Shot the steer with a rifle."

"Everett?" Virgil said.

"Sounds like somebody wanted you to know something," I said.

"Sign?" Virgil said.

"I was here," I said.

"Why would somebody want us to know?" Virgil said.

"Don't know," I said. "Fella who left it wouldn'ta known you had a tracker. Maybe he wanted you to know it was Comanche that slaughtered your cows."

"You go after them?" Virgil said.

"Nope, let 'em have the beef. Figured it

would keep them from bothering us any-more."

"And it did?"

Lester nodded.

"Guess so," Lester said. "There wasn't many of 'em, Garr says."

"And there's fifty-one of you," Virgil said.

"Yep, all with Winchesters."

"That mighta kept them from bothering you," Virgil said.

"Coulda been a factor," Lester said.

"You staying around after you pen the herd?" Virgil said.

"Nope. I'll stay for the tally. Then I'm on a train to Fort Worth. Take a bath, get drunk, find a woman, and do all of it by myself."

"Thanks for stopping by," Virgil said.

18

"Fellas bringing four thousand head a cattle into town tomorrow," Virgil said.

Pike nodded. He was leaning his elbows on his big, elegant bar. The heel of one boot hooked over the brass rail. It wasn't J.D. in the lookout chair today.

"Leave 'em at the station?" Pike said.

"Yep."

"Pay off the drovers?" Pike said.

"Uh-huh."

Pike looked over at the lookout.

"Looks like you and J.D. gonna be busy, Kirby."

"Might be," Kirby said.

Kirby was a big man with a thick, dark mustache and a bald head.

"Thought me 'n Everett would come by, let you know, see if you had a plan for dealing with any trouble might arise."

"Kind of you," Pike said. "You boys want a beer, or something with more muscle?"

"Beer's good," Virgil said.

"On the house," Pike said, and nodded at one of the bartenders.

"Any plan?" Virgil said.

"I'm grateful for your concern, Virgil."

"Well, there's fifty-one of them and two of us, so I'm making a, whatcha call it, Everett, what we're doing."

"We're making a tactical assessment," I said.

Pike nodded.

"See who can protect themselves," he said. "And who needs you two boys to do it."

"There you have it," Virgil said.

" 'Course, there may not be any trouble," Pike said.

"Maybe not," Virgil said.

"Not a lot of cowboys gonna cross Virgil Cole," Pike said.

Spec set beer on the bar in front of us.

"But I don't want to take no chance that some drunken vaquero with cow shit on his heels comes in here and busts up my beautiful Palace."

"Be a shame," Virgil said.

"Well, we'll have J.D. in the chair, and Kirby at the door. Spec here can do a little more than draw beer. I'll be here. And some of my other associates'll be draped around the room here, ready to, ah, intercede if the revelers get too lively."

"Called away from their normal duties," I said.

Pike grinned at me.

"Those are their normal duties," he said.

"Left over from the old days," I said.

"Some," Pike said.

"Okay, Pike," Virgil said. "You do what you need to do to protect yourself and your place."

"Be my plan," Pike said.

"And I'd appreciate it if you didn't do more than you had to," Virgil said.

"Don't see no reason to," Pike said.

19

All along Arrow Street it was pretty much the same. They'd had trail drives before.

"But nothing this size," I said to the manager at a saloon called The Cheyenne Gentleman's Bar.

"No," he said. "That's true. But we got Roy here."

He nodded at a hugely fat bouncer near the door.

"And I hear tell you boys know how to keep order."

We moved on.

"They don't get it," I said to Virgil. "They ain't never experienced forty-eight or so soused cattle drivers with cash in their pockets, blowing in all at once, with a big thirst and a fearsome hard-on."

"May not turn out to be so proud of all them extra cattle pens," Virgil said.

At a woman's clothing store, the owner spoke to Virgil.

"I believe I'll be closing," she said, "while those cowboys are loose in town. I don't sell things cowboys want anyway."

"Might have wives or girlfriends at home," Virgil said.

"They won't be buying things for the wife on their first night off the trail," the woman said. "Maybe the night they leave."

"Guilt?" I said.

"Guilt," she said.

Aside from the dress-shop lady, most of the places along Arrow Street were thinking less about damage and more about profit. Virgil's reputation probably accounted for a lot of that. None of them could imagine somebody standing up to him . . . assuming the standee knew his reputation.

We paused in front of The Church of the Brotherhood.

"Suppose Brother Percival got the same right to know as anybody else," Virgil said.

" 'Less God already told him," I said.

We walked up the steps and in through the pen doors. Inside, it was dim in its flint-blue way, and the organ was playing. We walked forward toward the altar and turned and looked up into the choir loft. It was Allie.

"Thought it sounded pretty bad," Virgil said.

"Loud, though," I said.

Virgil nodded.

"Well, she ain't singing," I said.

"Hallelujah," Virgil said.

Brother Percival strode gravely up the aisle.

"Isn't she wonderful?" he said, nodding at Allie above.

"Wonderful," Virgil said.

"She's practicing now," Percival said.

"Good," Virgil said.

"Pretty little woman," Percival said. "Been coming here every day for morning service. Last week she asked if she could try playing the organ. Now she plays every day."

"Big trail herd being delivered here tomorrow," Virgil said. "Town will be full of drunken cowboys."

"Why is that my concern?"

"Might cause some trouble," Virgil said.

"That should be your concern."

"Is," Virgil said. "Why I'm coming around . . . making a tactical assessment."

"We can take care of ourselves," Brother Percival said. "Ours is a muscular and militant Christianity."

"Being as Choctaw is one of your deacons, made me kind of suspect that," Virgil said.

"Deacon Brown is a fine church member," Percival said.

"Sure," Virgil said.

"And I can't believe these cowboys would invade a church," Percival said.

"Ain't likely," Virgil said.

"But if they should, we can and will defend ourselves."

"Only thing is," Virgil said, "if you got to defend yourself, I'd like to be sure that Choctaw don't get too militant and muscular."

"Deacon Brown, like all of us here in the congregation, will do what he must," Percival said.

"Don't we all," Virgil said.

"It is God's work," Percival said.

Virgil nodded and looked up in the choir loft where Allie was still laboring over the organ. I didn't recognize what she was playing.

"Hope so," Virgil said.

20

Abe Lester brought his herd in from the south, right after sunrise. He trailed them along the river so he wouldn't have to run them through town. At the pens they made a lot of noise and kicked up a lot of dust as the drovers herded them in. It took nearly all day to get them penned, and by midafternoon the dust was hanging over the town like smoke above a brush fire.

When Lester began to pay off the drovers, Virgil and I strolled down to observe.

"Every man taken care of his string, Spanish?" Lester said to a Mexican cowboy standing to the side.

"Sí," the vaquero said. "All in the remuda pen, been rubbed down, got feed and water."

We were in the tally shack at the pens. Lester was at a table with a big box in front of him. Virgil and I stood behind him. Both of us were wearing our badges. I was carrying the eight-gauge, which almost always got people's attention.

Before the first man stepped up to be paid, Virgil spoke.

"My name's Virgil Cole," he said. "Fella with the eight-gauge is Everett Hitch. We want to welcome you to Brimstone. We want you to have a hell of a good time in Brimstone. And we want you to do it without hurting anybody or breaking anything."

No one said anything.

Finally, Lester spoke.

"I pay you off," he said, "and you don't have no reason to do what I tell you anymore."

From the back of the line somebody gave a soft rebel yell. A couple of the men laughed.

"On the other hand," Lester said, "I got no obligation to help you out, you get in trouble. I assume some of you boys know who Virgil Cole is."

Nobody spoke.

"Okay," Lester said.

The drovers came up, one at a time, still sweating, with dust caked on their faces, and took their money. Several of them looked us over. None of them said anything. The Mexican wrangler was the last. With the money distributed and the box empty,

Lester closed the lid and stood.

"Good luck with them," he said.

Virgil nodded.

Lester put the box under his arm and walked out of the tally shed.

"Lotta cowboys," I said to Virgil.

"Yep."

"Don't seem a bad lot," I said.

"Yet," Virgil said.

"Some of them were heeled," I said. "Some weren't."

"Don't matter if they're heeled right now," Virgil said.

"I know," I said.

"Matter more tonight," Virgil said.

"What's your guess?" I said.

" 'Bout tonight?" Virgil said.

"Yeah," I said. "Think we'll have to kill one?"

"Might," Virgil said.

21

By midnight most of the drovers had settled in with a whore or passed out somewhere. Two of them were in our jail. Virgil and I walked along Arrow Street past The Church of the Brotherhood. It was dark and still.

"No cowboys," I said.

"No deacons, either," Virgil said.

"Guess the cowboys got other things to do," I said.

"Don't nobody seem much interested in the church," Virgil said. " 'Cept Allie."

"She goes a lot?" I said.

" 'Bout every day."

"That bad?" I said.

"Hell, no," Virgil said. "It's good. Otherwise, she'd be home cooking and washing. She's ruined half my shirts."

"She's trying," I said.

"She is," Virgil said.

"She's had a rough go," I said.

"Yep."

"S'pose she brought most of it on herself," I said.

"She did," Virgil said.

"Maybe the church will help her," I said.

"Hope so," Virgil said.

Arrow Street was mostly dark now. The shops were closed, and the saloons that were still open were quiet. Ahead, at the corner of Fifth and Arrow, a group of drovers was standing in the street. In the quiet I heard their voices.

"You got no business treating us like that, Pike."

As we got closer, I could see Pike standing on the boardwalk in front of the Palace.

"Ah, but I do, my friend," Pike said.

J.D. and Kirby stood on the boardwalk with him. All three wore Colts.

"You broke Charlie's arm," the cowboy said.

"I did," Pike said. "Keep yammering at me, I might break yours."

The door to the Palace opened and a fourth man came out wearing a gun.

"Choctaw," Virgil said to me.

He quickened his pace.

"He wasn't doin' anything," the cowboy said.

"He was messing up my saloon," Pike said. "I don't tolerate anybody messing up

100

my saloon."

"Well," the cowboy said, "we don't tolerate nobody hurting our friend."

The man's voice had risen. I could hear the whiskey in it.

But we weren't close enough.

"Well, then, my friend," Pike said. "You best make your move."

Virgil yelled, "Hold it."

But it was too late. The cowboy fumbled at his gun and a couple of men beside him did the same. Pike shot three of them before they got anywhere near clearing their holsters. One bullet each. The rest of the cowboys froze. J.D. and Kirby and Choctaw had their guns out but didn't shoot.

"Fast," I said.

"And eager," Virgil said.

Then he raised his voice.

"Everything stops," he said.

We were close enough now. The men stood poised and motionless, as if posing for a photograph.

Then Pike smiled and said, "Virgil."

I veered off across the street with the eight-gauge and stood behind the cowboys. Virgil stepped up onto the boardwalk.

"Seen you coming up the street," Pike said. "Glad you're here."

"You can put it away now," Virgil said.

Pike smiled some more.

"Glad to," he said.

He opened the cylinder of his Colt, ejected the three spent shells, added three fresh ones from his coat pocket, closed the cylinder, and slid the Colt softly into its holster.

"You saw him pull on me," Pike said.

"I did," Virgil said.

"And those other boys," Pike said.

"Yep."

"They pulled on me, too," Pike said cheerfully.

"And you shot three drunks," Virgil said.

"That made it easier," Pike said.

The cowboys had gathered silently around the three dead men. None of them knew what to do.

"They're dead," Virgil said to the cowboys. "There's an undertaker down past the livery corral on Second Street. One of you go roust him out. Tell him I want him up here."

The cowboys stared at Virgil and looked at the dead men in the street and at one another. Then they began, as a group, as if for mutual support, to drift on down toward the livery.

"Fella with the broken arm," Virgil said. "There's a doctor right next to the undertaker."

Pike grinned.

"Convenient," Pike said.

Virgil turned back to the men on the boardwalk.

"You all seen it the same way," he said.

"We did," J.D. said.

Kirby nodded. Virgil looked at Choctaw. Choctaw met his gaze silently.

" 'Course you did," Virgil said.

The three men went back inside the Palace, leaving Virgil and Pike on the boardwalk. I came across the street and joined them.

"Good to see you, Everett," Pike said.

I nodded. Everything was quiet. And except for us and the three dead men bleeding in the street, the town seemed empty.

"Pretty quiet night," Pike said. "All things considered."

"Pretty quick with that Colt," I said.

"I am," Pike said. "Good you come along when you done."

"Yeah, you mighta shot 'em all," I said.

"Mighta had to," Pike said.

"Four gun hands against a bunch of drunks," I said.

"Drunks with guns," Pike said. "A lucky shot will kill you just as dead."

I nodded.

"I got no problem killing people. No more than you fellas. Done it before. Probably do it again. But these boys pulled on me."

"They did," Virgil said. "You ain't broke no law."

"Good," Pike said with a wide smile. "Musta been a long night for you boys. Have a drink on me?"

"No thanks," Virgil said.

"Offer stands," Pike said. "Good talking with you boys."

He turned and went back into the Palace.

"Don't seem too upset," I said to Virgil as we walked up toward the sheriff's office.

"Nope," Virgil said.

"Too bad we didn't get here a little sooner," I said.

"Too bad," Virgil said.

We unlocked the sheriff's office and went in. The two drunks were still asleep in their cells. I leaned the eight-gauge in the corner. Virgil sat and put his feet up on the desk.

"Choctaw," Virgil said. "Wonder what Choctaw was doing there."

22

The sun was shining. The streets were quiet. The town was back in rhythm. Brother Percival and his followers were holding forth outside of a saloon called The Silver Bullet. Virgil and I stood across the street watching. There were eight or ten of the faithful outside the saloon, and anytime someone wanted to go in or out, they had to push through the crowd of Percivalians and listen to warnings of eternal hellfire and lifelong shame. Leaning against the wall of the saloon, just behind the group, was Choctaw Brown.

"This is hell's mouth," Percival bellowed. "Inside this door, women give up their womanhood for money. Inside this door, men trade their manhood for whiskey. Inside this door begins the slippery, desperate slide to hell."

The church members with him chanted, "Amen, brother." And no one chanted it as loudly as Allie. Most of the men pushing in and out paid very little attention, looking at the ground as they eased through among the prayers of the vigilant. One man was jostled as he went through them, and, annoyed, shoved Brother Percival as he went past. Percival took hold of his shirt front and picked him up and threw him into the street.

"Do not put your hands on a man of God!" Brother Percival said.

It wasn't a bellow. It was like the soft growl of a mountain lion. The man in the street gathered himself for a moment and then stood up and took a knife from his boot.

"You sonovabitch," he said.

Virgil and I started across the street. Choctaw stepped away from the door and in front of Brother Percival. He didn't draw his gun, but his hand hovered over it. He said nothing. The man with the knife looked at Choctaw, and past him at Percival.

"Choctaw," Virgil said.

Choctaw nodded faintly.

"Hold the knife," Virgil said.

The man with the knife stopped and looked back at Virgil.

"Aw," the man with the knife said. "Fuck it."

106

He turned and walked away down the street, with the knife still in his hand, dangling by his side as he went. Virgil was still looking at Choctaw. Choctaw had no expression as he looked back at Virgil.

"Virgil," Allie said. "Everything's fine now."

She stepped away from the group and put her hands on Virgil's chest and looked up at him.

"Everything's fine," she said. "Please."

Virgil was looking past her at Choctaw. Then he nodded.

"Sure," he said.

He turned away from her and walked down the street in the same direction that the man with the knife had gone.

"Keep your hands off the civilians," I said to Brother Percival.

"I answer to God," Percival said. "Not to you."

"Long as you are in this town," I said, "you answer to me and Virgil."

Choctaw Brown grunted.

"Don't blaspheme," Brother Percival said.

"Please, Everett," Allie said. "We're only trying to help people save their souls. I'm trying to save my soul."

I looked down at her. She had her hands flat on my chest now, looking up at me, just as she had looked up at Virgil.

"Perhaps you should consider your own soul," Brother Percival said.

I grinned at him.

"Too late," I said. "Right, Choctaw?"

Choctaw made a small derisive sound. No one else said anything. I patted Allie on the cheek and left. As I walked down Arrow Street I heard Allie leading her colleagues in singing a hymn I didn't recognize. I didn't know whether I failed to recognize it because it was not a hymn I knew or because they sang it so badly it was unrecognizable.

I walked a little faster.

23

The drovers were gone. The cattle had been shipped. There wasn't all that much for me and Virgil to do except sit in a couple of chairs, tilted back against the wall, outside the office, and watch what passed before us. It was a hot morning, with a high sky and an occasional white cloud. Freight wagons moved slowly up Arrow Street. The railroad surrey shuttled between the hotel and the railroad station. Women and children went in and out of shops. A few men, starting early, went in and out of the saloons.

"What do you think 'bout Allie," Virgil said.

"She's looking good again," I said. "Filled out nice."

Virgil nodded, looking at the street.

"You see her at the house," Virgil said. "Cooks our supper, serves it, won't sit down herself."

"Yep."

"Cleans up afterwards," Virgil said. "Don't say nothing."

"True," I said.

"Does the wash, irons, cleans . . ."

"I know," I said.

"Like last night, she's serving supper, and I say to her, 'Why don't you sit down and join us, Allie?' And she don't."

"I know," I said. "I was there, too."

"When she ain't cleaning and sewing and fucking up my shirts, and cooking bad," Virgil said, "she's reading the Bible, or she's in church, or she's sashaying down to the saloons to save souls with Brother Percival."

"I know."

"She was outside the Paiute Club yesterday evening, telling everybody she had defilled herself for money."

"Defiled," I said.

"Defiled."

"Virgil," I said. "Why you telling me all this. I know all this."

"I ain't telling you nothing," Virgil said. "I'm discussing it with you."

"Oh," I said.

"Why don't she settle down," Virgil said. "Be like she used to be."

"Maybe she don't want to be like she used to be," I said.

"Well, no," Virgil said. "Maybe not the bad

parts. But . . ." He shook his head. "You know, she used to be a lotta fun."

"Sometimes," I said. "You and she doing anything in bed?"

"Nope."

"Why not?"

"I don't want to," Virgil said.

"Ever?"

"Don't know 'bout ever," Virgil said. "Don't want to right now."

"She mind that?" I said.

"Don't know," Virgil said. "She don't say nothing 'bout it."

"The Allie I know would mind," I said.

Virgil shook his head slightly.

"So, what's she trying to be now," he said, "if she don't want to be what she was?"

"Maybe she's trying to be a good woman."

"She thinks this is what a good woman's like?" Virgil said.

"Don't know what she thinks," I said. "She ain't had much experience with good women, maybe."

"And you have?"

"Hell, no," I said. "I don't know no good women."

"Me either," Virgil said.

"How about the lady in Resolution?" I said.

"Beth Redmond," he said. "She was really

a good woman, she wouldn't have cheated on her husband."

"With you," I said.

"That's right."

"Maybe the husband was a bad man," I said.

"He weren't much," Virgil said.

"She was a pretty nice woman," I said.

"Yeah," Virgil said. "She was."

"Went back to her husband," I said.

"She did."

"Stood by him."

Virgil nodded, still looking at the movement of life on Arrow Street.

"Don't explain Allie," he said.

"Nope."

Virgil grinned at me.

"Don't explain me, neither," he said.

"Not sure what would," I said.

24

A teamster with his collar up came into the sheriff's office just as it started to rain. He told us there was a dead man two miles south of town, on the river road, and he thought it was Indians.

"We'll take a look," Virgil said.

"Ain't you gonna get a posse?" he said.

"Me and Everett'll go," Virgil said, and got up and got a Winchester, put on his slicker, and put a box of bullets in the pocket.

I took the eight-gauge.

The horses were very lively from standing around too long at the livery. But after the first mile they settled down in the cool rain, which was now coming pretty steady. The river had cut deep into the land along here, with banks maybe twenty feet high. As we topped a rise we saw the wagon, and on the wagon seat was a man with an arrow in his stomach. We stopped the horses. Virgil scanned the area. It was flat at the bottom of the rise and went flat for a long distance along this side of the river. There was no one in sight. We rode on down.

There were no horses with the wagon, and no cargo. Just the dead man on the wagon seat with the arrow sticking out.

"Musta stole the horses," Virgil said.

"Maybe why they killed him," I said. "For the horses."

We dismounted and took a look.

"Didn't bleed much," I said.

"Did in the back," Virgil said.

I reached up and pulled the arrow out. It hadn't gone in very deeply.

"No arrowhead," I said.

"Think it pulled loose?"

"No," I said. "It's just a sharpened stick with some feathers on the shaft."

Virgil jumped into the bed of the wagon and examined the man's back.

"Didn't need no arrowhead," Virgil said. "Man's been shot at least twice."

"So, what's the arrow for?" I said.

"Maybe somebody just stuck it in him after he was dead," Virgil said.

"Like that steer that Lester found?" I said.

"You done a lot of Indian fighting," Virgil said. "You tell what kind of arrow that is?"

"They make 'em out of what they can

find," I said. "So they ain't all the same. Nothing to say it ain't Comanche."

"Most of 'em got rifles now, don't they?" Virgil said.

"Yep. Bows and arrows are mostly sentimental," I said. "Like a tradition."

"Why no arrowhead?" Virgil said.

"They're hard to make; nobody want to waste them," I said.

"And he didn't need to," Virgil said. " 'Cause he already shot the guy dead, 'fore the arrow went in."

"I'd say it's a kid's arrow, I had to guess. They give them blunt arrows and small bows to play with. Can practice with them and don't hurt themselves. I'd say this fella took a kid's arrow and sharpened it up and stuck it in."

Virgil nodded.

"So it may be a sign, like Abe Lester's steer," he said.

"Don't know why else you'd do it," I said.

He got down from the wagon and looked at the ground.

"You read sign better than I do," Virgil said. "You make anything outta this?"

I looked at the muddy muddle around the wagon.

"All I can make out is that it's raining hard," I said.

115

"Hell," Virgil said. "I figured that out."

I straightened up. Virgil was standing stock-still, looking through the rain across the river, which was maybe two hundred yards wide here. I looked, too.

There was a big Indian sitting on a smallish paint horse, watching us. He appeared to be wearing buckskin leggings and moccasins, and a long black cloak and a big wide-brimmed black hat like the Quakers wear. The hat was pulled down low on his head. He had a rifle in a fringed rifle scabbard balanced across the horse's shoulders in front of him. He didn't move.

"Can't get across," I said. " 'Less he's willin' to wait while we find a place to ford."

Virgil didn't say anything. He kept looking at the Indian.

"And a'course if he's willing to wait for us," I said, "who else is waiting behind the swale over there."

Virgil and the Indian kept looking at each other. I wondered if the Indian knew that Virgil would know him twenty years from now if he saw him again. On the other hand, maybe the Indian would know Virgil, too.

"You could probably shoot him from here," I said. "Bein' as how you're Virgil Cole and all."

"He ain't done nothing," Virgil said.

"Might have," I said.

"Can't shoot a man for sitting on his horse."

"Hell, Virgil, he's an Indian," I said. "Mighta killed this poor fella and stole his horses."

"Can't shoot a man for sitting on his horse," Virgil said again.

"What are we gonna do about the dead gentleman," I said.

"Wagon's too heavy for our two horses," Virgil said. "And he's starting to smell. We'll go get the undertaker."

"And leave him here?" I said.

"He ain't in no hurry," Virgil said.

"I suppose he ain't," I said.

We mounted up and turned the horses back toward town with the river on our left. The Indian turned his horse and rode along with us.

"He stays with us to the edge of town, there's a ford," I said.

"He'll be gone by the time we reach the ford," Virgil said.

And he was.

25

The undertaker repaired the dead man enough for us to display him outside the undertaker's shop. People came to look at him and before noon we knew who he'd been. His name was Peter Lussier. Worked on a spread ten miles down the Paiute. No wife. No kids. He'd been on his way into town to buy supplies for the cook shack.

"Wonder why that Indian spent so much time showing himself to us?" Virgil said.

"Don't know," I said.

"Them red beasties can be strange," Virgil said.

"They ain't as strange as we like to think they are," I said. "They got reasons for what they do, just like us. Except sometimes they don't."

"Just like us," Virgil said.

"Yep."

Virgil drank some coffee.

"Every morning," he said, "Allie comes

down here and makes us coffee and leaves, and we throw it away and make some new coffee."

I nodded.

"Whadda you think of that?" Virgil said.

"Better than drinking hers," I said.

"A'course," Virgil said. "But don't you think there's something wrong with it?"

"Sure," I said.

"But she's trying to translate herself," Virgil said. "You know, make herself different?"

"Transform," I said.

"That's right," Virgil said. "She's trying to transform herself."

"And you don't want to tell her it ain't working," I said.

"Well, maybe it is," Virgil said. "Except she can't make coffee."

"Or sew or iron or wash clothes," I said. "Or cook."

"Hell," Virgil said. "She can't sing and play the piano, either, but she been doing it for years."

"I thought you liked her piano playing," I said.

"God, no," Virgil said. "You?"

"No," I said. "Singing, neither."

It was still raining, and the water ran down the windows in the front of the office, changing the shape of everything moving in the street. Virgil sipped his coffee and looked at the rain.

"She used to be fun," Virgil said. "Now she working so hard to make it up to me, she ain't fun anymore."

"She is pretty drab," I said.

"Drab," Virgil said.

"Sorta no color," I said. "Boring."

He nodded.

"Drab," he said. "That's her. Drab."

"Maybe if you was to say something to her."

Virgil shook his head.

"Know the only thing she's good at?" Virgil said.

"Not firsthand," I said.

Virgil nodded.

"She's good at it," Virgil said.

I nodded.

"Built for it," he said.

"I notice she's filled back out, since we come here," I said.

"She has," Virgil said.

"But . . ." I said.

"Ain't ready yet," Virgil said.

"Why not?" I said.

"Got to think it through," Virgil said.

"You love her?"

"That's what I'm thinking through," Virgil said.

"We come all the way down here looking for her," I said. "And killed four men to get her out of Placido, and you don't know if you love her."

"Thought I did when we come down here," Virgil said.

"But?"

"But I can't seem to get past what she done yet," Virgil said.

"The men or the running off, or both."

"Understand the running off," Virgil said. "She felt shamed. But the other men."

"It didn't work out for her," I said. "You seen where we found her."

"No," Virgil said. "And I don't have no problem with the whoring when she didn't have no choice. Feel bad for her. But I don't have no problem."

"Bragg?" I said.

"Him, the other men, when she had a choice."

"Maybe she thinks she didn't," I said.

"Then what she transforming for?" Virgil said.

"Please you?"

"It don't please me."

"And you ain't talked about it," I said.

"Can't," Virgil said.

I nodded.

"Neither one of us," Virgil said.

I nodded again.

"Yet," Virgil said.

26

When Allie brought our lunch, Virgil and I were sitting outside the sheriff's office watching the last of the whiskey get packed onto a wagon, in front of the Bluebell Saloon.

"Isn't that good?" Allie said.

"The Bluebell?" Virgil said.

"Yes, it's closing. They're going away."

"Some saloons left," Virgil said.

"Not so many," Allie said. "Brother Percival says we've driven four of them out already."

"Pike's Palace still doing well, though," Virgil said.

I knew why he said it. He was still thinking about Choctaw Brown being with Pike the night Pike killed three men. Virgil never forgot anything, and he never let anything go.

"Brother Percival says Mr. Pike is running a much more Christian enterprise than the others."

Virgil said, "Uh-huh."

"I think they're actually kind of friends," Allie said. "I see them together sometimes."

Virgil nodded.

"What's Pike do that the others don't?" Virgil said.

"I don't really know," Allie said. "But I know Brother Percival sends some of the deacons over there regularly."

"How 'bout Deacon Brown?" Virgil said.

"Yes, he goes over."

"And they go there to make sure," I said, "that he's running a Christian saloon."

Allie's face sort of squeezed in on itself.

She said, "Being Christian doesn't mean being foolish, Everett. We know men have their needs."

She looked at the floor.

"Women, too, I guess," she said. "And we don't expect everyone to be perfect. So we are working to get rid of the worst kind of vice dens, and try to maintain a better option."

"Why not let them decide for themselves," I said.

Allie didn't look at either of us. She stared down the street and watched the wagon pull away from the Bluebell.

"People can't always decide for themselves. When they do, many times they decide the wrong thing."

Neither Virgil nor I said anything.

"And they can't ever make it up," Allie said. "They try and try, but the thing they did was too wrong . . . and they can't fix it."

"Nothing can't be fixed," Virgil said.

Allie turned her head toward him. She didn't speak for a time. Virgil didn't say anything else.

"You really believe that, Virgil?"

"I do," he said.

They looked silently at each other. Allie opened her mouth to speak and closed it without speaking. They looked some more.

Then Allie said, "Here's your lunch. I got to go practice on the organ now."

She handed the lunch basket to Virgil, who took it.

He said, "Thank you, Allie."

She nodded and smiled sort of uncertainly, and then turned and headed south on Arrow Street toward the church. Virgil watched her go.

"Something up between Percival and Pike," Virgil said.

"That what we was talking about?" I said.

"Partly," Virgil said.

27

The house was little more than a cabin, with a stock shed next to it. In front of it, in the trampled dirt yard, was a dead man face-down with part of his head blown off. An arrow protruded from his back below the ribs. In the stock shed, a milk cow was making some noise.

Virgil and I dismounted and went into the house. There were three rooms. All of them empty.

"There's women's clothes in both bedrooms," I said to Virgil. "But no women."

"And there's a wagon and a plow in the yard but no horses," Virgil said.

"Somebody took 'em both?"

"Maybe our Indian friend," Virgil said.

We went back into the yard and squatted on our heels beside the body. I shooed the flies away and pulled out the arrow.

"Same kind of arrow," I said. "No point."

The cow was still complaining in the shed.

"Needs to be milked," Virgil said.

"Sounds that way," I said.

"You know how to do that?" Virgil said.

"Nope."

"I do," Virgil said, and went to the shed.

The cow was in one stall; the other two stalls were empty. Virgil found a milking stool and began to milk the cow, letting the milk soak into the hard earth of the shed.

"Shame to waste it," I said.

"Cow don't think so," Virgil said.

While he milked the cow I studied what little sign there was on the hard-packed earth. When Virgil was through, he pitched some hay from the loft into the feed trough, and left the shed gate open.

"We'll take her back to town when we go," Virgil said. "Maybe Allie can do something with her."

"Can't read much here," I said. "Ground's too hard. But over there, leading toward the river, there's the tracks of maybe three horses. Two of them probably shod, one of them not. I think."

We stood together over the dead body.

"Killed the man," Virgil said. "Took the horses and the women."

"A while ago," I said.

"He is getting kind of ripe," Virgil said.

127

"We don't smell good when we're dead," I said.

"Especially after a while," Virgil said.

"Probably don't care, though."

"Probably don't," Virgil said.

He was looking off in the direction where the hoof prints led.

"Got a start on us," Virgil said.

"Yep, but if he's traveling with two women," I said, "he might be going slower than we will."

Virgil glanced suddenly over his shoulder back toward town. I could see dust rising along the road from town, and in another minute I heard the sound of horses and a wagon.

"Be the undertaker," Virgil said. "He can take the body. We'll take the cow."

28

Virgil was feeding shells into his Winchester when Pike came into the sheriff's office with a dark, lean, hard-looking man.

"Virgil," Pike said. "Everett."

We both nodded.

"This here's Pony Flores," Pike said. "One of my employees."

"From the old days?" I said.

Pike nodded.

"Old days," he said.

Virgil and I both nodded at Flores. He nodded back.

"Understand some Indians killed Tom Ostermueller, and took his wife and daughter."

"Something like that," Virgil said.

"You going after them?"

"Yep."

"Posse?"

"Nope."

"Posse'd just get in the way," Pike said.

"It would," Virgil said.

"Bunch of townspeople with guns," Pike said.

"Probably shoot their own horse, they ever have to clear a weapon," Virgil said.

"Lend you some of mine," Pike said.

Virgil shook his head.

"Me 'n Everett will do," he said.

"Got a tracker?" Pike said.

"Everett can track some," Virgil said.

"Pony can track a butterfly two days after," Pike said.

Virgil looked at me.

"Where'd you learn to track?" I said.

"Apache," Flores said.

"Pony's mother is Apache," Pike said.

"Chiricahua," Flores said.

"That your real name?" Virgil said.

Pony shook his head and said something in Apache.

"Means what?" Virgil said.

There was a brief expression on Pony's face that might have been amusement.

"Pony Running," I said.

"Okay if we stick with Pony?" Virgil said to Flores.

"Okay."

"Father's Mexican," Pike said.

"Can he talk for himself?" Virgil said.

Pike smiled.

"Try him," Pike said.

"Live with your mother's people?" I said.

"Some."

"Track as good as Pike says?"

"Yes."

"Speak English okay?" I said.

"Speak it good," Pony said.

"Just not often," Virgil said.

Pony looked like he might have smiled for a moment, but he didn't say anything.

"Speak Spanish?"

"Sí."

"Any Comanche?"

"A little bit," Pony said.

"Shoot?" Virgil said.

"I can shoot," Pony said.

"Will you?"

"Sure."

"Why do you want to track for us?" I said.

"Two women," Pony said.

"You know them?"

"No."

"But you want to help us save them," I said.

"Yes."

Virgil and I looked at each other.

"He's good," Pike said. "Been with me a long time."

"Good how?" Virgil said.

"Colt, Winchester, knife," Pike said. "Best tracker I ever saw."

"Keep his word?" Virgil said.

"I do," Pony said.

Virgil looked at me.

"Everett?" he said.

"He can probably track better than I can," I said. "What I learned I learned from Apache scouts."

Virgil nodded.

"Okay," he said. "I can pay you half a dollar a day. You supply your own horse and saddle, your own weapons and ammunition."

"Yes," Pony said.

29

We said good-bye to Allie on the front porch of the house we were renting. It was just after sunrise, and she was barefoot and in her nightgown. She and Virgil put their arms around each other. But they didn't kiss, and when he stepped back and swung up onto his horse, she smiled at me and patted my cheek.

"Take care of each other," she said.

I got up on my horse.

"Have somebody milk that cow every day," Virgil said.

"I will," she said.

None of us moved. Virgil looked down from the saddle at Allie.

"I'll come back," he said.

Then he wheeled the horse and I followed with the pack mule on a lead, and we rode up Third Street toward Arrow. Pony was mounted and waiting outside Pike's Palace, and he swung in beside us as we rode south

out of town. We stopped at the Ostermueller farm shack. Pony got down and spent
maybe ten minutes looking at the ground,
then mounted his horse and led us out
toward the river where the tracks led.

Once we were into the open, I took the
mule off the lead. He'd follow the horses,
and if he didn't, one of us could haze him
back.

"You see more than one Indian?" I said.

"No," Pony said.

"And two shod," I said.

"Yes."

"Tell if anyone's riding the shod horses?"

"Need to see tracks when no one rides
them, and tracks when someone does,"
Pony said.

We rode south along the river most of the
day. Pony rode quietly, looking at the tracks.
Occasionally he would lean out of the
saddle and study them, then he would re-
sume.

"Don't seem worried 'bout covering his
tracks," Virgil said.

"No," Pony said. "But he don't know I
the one following."

Virgil grinned.

"Figures we can't track?" he said.

"Yes," Pony said.

We came to a ford at the end of the day,

134

and the tracks led into it. The sun was down, and it was hard to see the bank on the other side of the river.

"Might want to camp this side," Virgil said. "Kinda hate to get caught in the middle of the river in the near dark by a man with a rifle."

"We can cross in the morning," Pony said.

We made a fire and cooked some bacon and beans. I took a jug from the pack, and we passed it around while the supper cooked.

"How long you work for Pike?" I said to Pony.

"Since wild times," Pony said.

"Outlaw times," I said.

"Yes."

"Always the way he is now?"

"Sure," Pony said.

"Big, friendly bear," Virgil said. "Everybody's friend."

"Sure."

" 'Cept when he ain't," Virgil said.

Pony frowned for a moment, translating Virgil's remark into whatever language he thought in.

"You mean when he kill people," Pony said.

"Uh-huh."

"He like to kill people," Pony said.

"I know," Virgil said.

Pony took a pull on the bottle.

"You no like that," he said.

"Don't mind it," Virgil said.

Pony handed me the bottle.

"You ever fight with us when you was living Apache?" I said.

Pony smiled.

"Blue Dogs?" he said. "Sure, I fight."

"I was a Blue Dog," I said.

Pony nodded.

"Maybe we fought each other," I said.

"Maybe," Pony said.

"Does it matter?" I said.

"When I with Apache," he said, "I tell them I fight for them, and I do. Now I with you. I tell you I fight for you. I will fight."

"Even against another Indian?" I said.

"I am also Mexican," Pony said, and almost smiled again. "And this man who has stolen the ladies. He not Chiricahua."

"How do you know?" I said.

Virgil had the whiskey bottle. He took a drink and passed it on to Pony. Pony drank some and looked at me and might have smiled.

"No Chiricahua around here," he said.

30

In the morning we sat our horses at the ford, looking across the river. There was nothing to see.

"I go," Pony said.

"Why you?" I said.

"Tracker," Pony said.

He turned his horse and went into the river. It was shallow. The horse never had to swim. On the other side, Pony rode up the little rise, bending over to study the tracks. He pulled up at the top of the rise and looked around. Then he gestured for us to come. Virgil went in and then me, hazing the mule ahead of me.

Pony pointed when we reached him.

"Go off there," he said.

And he headed west. The tracks were still clear enough. I could follow them fine. But a mile or so from the river the land began to rise, and the footing became rockier. It was harder to see the tracks. But Pony stayed with it. He was maybe fifty yards ahead of us, near a cluster of boulders, when he stopped. Virgil pulled his horse to the right. I went left. The mule didn't know who to follow, so he just stood. I had the eight-gauge across my saddle, with both hammers back. We walked the horses slowly around the boulders until we met on the other side of them and were looking at Pony. The mule saw us together and trotted toward us.

I let the hammers down.

"What?" Virgil said.

"More horses," Pony said.

He pointed to the ground. There was a mingling of tracks, some of them leading behind the rocks.

"Nobody there," Virgil said.

Pony nodded and got off his horse. He squatted and looked at the tracks for a while. Then he stood and walked along, looking at the ground, around the boulders, and up the hill behind them. Virgil and I waited.

"Shod horses," I said.

"Yep."

"Can't say for sure how many."

"Pony will know," Virgil said.

"Could be white men," I said.

"Could be white men's horses that some Indians stole," Virgil said.

"Could be," I said.

"Maybe Pony can figure that out," Virgil said.

"Maybe not," I said.

We waited for maybe an hour while Pony looked at the ground.

"Five white men," he said.

Virgil smiled.

"How you know they're white?" he said.

"Boot prints," Pony said. "Comanche not wear boots."

"They have to be Comanche?" I said.

"Comanche land," Pony said. "They Indians, they Comanche."

"But they're not Indians," Virgil said.

"No," Pony said. "White. Five of them come from south. Stay here, build a fire, cook something. Like they waiting. Our people come in here."

He pointed to the tracks we'd been following.

"Get off horses," Pony said. "Man in moccasins, two women. Small footprints. Shoes not like man."

We followed. With Pony pointing it out, we could see what he saw. I wasn't sure I'd have seen it without him.

"Then everybody get on horse. All go south, except Indian. He go up the hill and into a canyon. Very stony. Hard to track."

"Could you?" Virgil said.

"Yes."

Virgil nodded.

"Women went south with the white men," he said.

"They were waiting here for him," I said.

"He sold them," Virgil said.

I nodded.

Virgil looked up the hill for a time.

Then he said, "We got to get them women back."

"Yes," I said.

"You sure they went with the white men," Virgil said.

"Sure," Pony said. "See horse tracks. They horses' feet, much bigger."

"Wagon horses," I said.

Pony got back up on his horse, and we headed south.

31

For two days we rode southwest, away from the river, into much rougher country. It made the tracking harder and slowed us down. But Pony kept the trail and told us it was getting fresher. We stopped at sundown on the third day on some high rocky ground at the edge of an arroyo and started to set up camp.

Pony had collected some brush for a fire, and as he set it down, he paused and raised his head, like a hunting dog with a scent. Virgil and I were still.

Then Virgil said, "Smoke."

Pony nodded. I sniffed at the air and didn't smell it, and didn't smell it, and then I did.

"Be surprising if it weren't them," Virgil said.

There was grass growing on the slope of the arroyo, and the animals were busy with it. They weren't likely to make any noise. It was dark, but there was moonlight and all the stars. Virgil picked up his Winchester, Pony took his, and I brought the eight-gauge, and we went very quietly along the arroyo to where the land sloped down. At the foot of the slope we could see a campfire and some people around it.

"Dumb place to camp," I said softly.

"They been riding what, four days?" Virgil said. "Ain't seen a soul. If they thought we was following, they figure we lost them when we left the river and the tracking got hard."

"Almost Mexico," Pony said.

"Probably where they're headed," Virgil said. "They think they're home free."

"And they ain't," I said.

"They're in range from here, 'cept for the eight-gauge," Virgil said.

"Can't make out who's who," I said.

"Pony?" Virgil said.

"Too far," Pony said.

"Be a hell of a thing," Virgil said. "We come all this way to save them women, and shoot 'em by mistake."

We were quiet, looking at the layout.

"We're really careful," Virgil said, "we can slither on down behind that outcropping and get a better look."

"Still too long a shot for the eight-gauge,"

142

I said. "Lemme get my rifle."

"While you're there," Virgil said, "make sure them animals is tethered. Don't want 'em running off soon's we start shooting."

I got my Winchester, checked the tethers, and walked softly back to where Virgil and Pony were lying on the ground, looking down at the camp.

"Jack a shell up into the chamber," Virgil said. "Do it when we get closer and they might hear it."

We did as he said, and eased the hammers off. Then, on our bellies, trying to be silent, we crawled and slithered our way downhill over the shale-littered ground to the rocks, halfway to the camp. All of us were scraped and bloody by the time we got there.

The five men looked to be Mexican. The two women sat close to each other, away from them to the left.

"Can't ride in among 'em," Virgil said. "Or walk in, for that matter. All them rocks underfoot, make too much noise going down the hill."

Neither Pony nor I said anything. We both knew Virgil wasn't talking to us. The men were passing a bottle around. The women were still.

"Okay," Virgil said. "Pony, can you shoot one of those fellas from here without hitting the women?"

"Yes."

"Okay, then we'll shoot the first three, left to right from the women. I'll take the closest one, fella in the hat. Everett takes the next one, with the striped shirt. Pony shoots the third one, buckskin shirt."

Virgil was silent. Neither Pony nor I said anything.

"Then I'll shoot the fella in the black vest," Virgil said, "and Everett, you and Pony shoot the other one. Fella with the beard. Recognize each one of them. Even if they get up and move around before we start shooting, you fire at the one I said."

Pony murmured, "Sí, jefe."

I said, "Yep."

"We don't shoot if we lose sight of anybody," Virgil said.

He cocked the Winchester. Pony and I did the same.

"You're sure there's only five," Virgil said. "I don't want there to be some fella out taking a leak to get ruckused up and shoot them women, 'fore we kill him."

"There are five, jefe," Pony said.

"Okay," Virgil said. "Pick out your target, get him in your sights."

All three of us took aim.

"Know who you're going to shoot, and

who you're gonna shoot next," Virgil said.

We waited. I had the middle button on the man's striped shirt sitting on top of my sight.

"Ready?" Virgil whispered.

Pony said, "Ready."

I took a deep breath and let it out.

I said, "Ready."

Virgil said, "Fire!" and I squeezed the trigger. It all moved at the stately pace these things always seemed to. I barely heard the shots. I saw my man go down, and as I shifted to the man with the beard, I levered another round up into the chamber and settled on his chest. He was leaning forward, frozen maybe, by the shock of the surprise, looking for a place to hide. There was no place to hide. I shot him in the chest and saw his body jerk as Pony shot him, too. Beside me, Virgil was on his feet and slip-sliding down the slope toward the campsite. Pony and I followed him. The two women were flat on the ground, one on top of the other.

When we reached the campfire, Virgil took out his Colt and put a bullet through the head of the first man he passed.

"They're dead," he said, and walked to the women. "But make sure."

Pony and I shot the other four men once

each in the head. The smell of gunfire was strong when we finished.

Virgil was sitting on his heels beside the two women. They were still huddled, one on top of the other.

"We come to rescue you," he said. "My name is Virgil Cole. I'm a deputy sheriff in Val Verde County, and the big fella is a deputy, too. His name is Everett Hitch. The slim gentleman is Pony Flores. He's our tracker. He's the one found you."

The women didn't move or speak. The one on top was older.

"I know you been through hell," Virgil said. "We'll take you up the hill to our camp, and feed you and let you sleep, and tomorrow we'll take you home."

The woman on top began to cry, harsh, ugly sounds that seemed to hurt as they came out. The woman underneath neither moved nor spoke. She still clung to the older woman.

"No rush," Virgil said. "When you're ready."

She was still making the retching sobbing sound, but the woman looked at Virgil, and seemed to see him, and nodded her head.

"Everett," Virgil said. "Whyn't you boys saddle up a couple horses, so these ladies don't have to walk up the hill."

32

At the top of the hill, they were both silent as we built up the campfire and gave them some blankets. Pony made fresh coffee. I got out some cups and the whiskey jug.

It was hard to tell what they might have looked like when they were living on the farm. What was left of them was pretty straggly. The older one had red hair, and some freckles. There was the hint of plumpness vanished about her. As if she had been full-figured and lost weight during her ordeal. The girl was blonde and smaller. Half developed. More than a girl, still less than a woman. They were dirty. Their clothes were barely clothes. And they were enveloped in a glaze of terror, which made them almost unrecognizable.

"Would you like some coffee?" I said to the older woman.

She nodded.

"Whiskey in it?" I said.

She nodded again.

"How 'bout the young lady?" I said.

The young lady had no reaction. The older woman nodded. I poured coffee and whiskey into both cups and handed one to each of them. The older woman blew on the surface of the coffee, and drank some. The young woman took a careful sip, and showed no reaction.

After her second cup, the older woman began to speak. Her voice was half swallowed, and she spoke very fast. They were mother and daughter. The mother's name was Mary Beth. The kid was Laurel. Mary Beth was thirty-seven. Laurel was fifteen. They both looked a lot older.

"My husband walked out the front door and the Indian shot him," Mary Beth said. "Didn't say anything, just shot him and stuck that arrow in him, then he made Laurel and me get on our horses and go with him, never even looked at my husband again, just made us ride away with him. At night he made us . . . do things with him . . . both of us right in front of each other, and he said we should get used to it because he was going to sell us to some men who would take us to Mexico . . ."

She stopped and drank from her cup. Laurel said nothing; she sipped at her coffee. The two women were wrapped in blankets. They sat close to the fire, more, I thought, for light than warmth. Virgil still sat on his heels beside them. Neither woman ever took her eyes off him.

"And then they came and took us and . . ."

She looked at her daughter. Her daughter's face was blank, her eyes fixed on Virgil. She drank more.

"You don't need to talk about it," Virgil said.

She nodded.

"Anything you can tell me 'bout this Indian?" Virgil said.

"He . . ." She drank again. "English. He talked good English."

Virgil nodded.

"And he was big; he was a very big Indian," Mary Beth said.

"What did he wear," Virgil said.

"Black coat," Mary Beth said. "Long. And a funny hat."

Virgil nodded. Mary Beth was drunk. Laurel seemed unchanged.

"Buffalo Calf," Mary Beth said.

"Buffalo Calf?" Virgil said.

"He said name Buffalo Calf."

Virgil nodded again. He glanced at Pony; Pony shrugged and shook his head.

We were quiet for a time. Outside the

149

circle of firelight, one of the horses stirred.

"Oh, God," Mary Beth said.

"Just one of the horses," Virgil said.

"But what if they come back?"

"Can't," Virgil said. "They're all dead."

"You kill them," Mary Beth said.

"We did."

"What if the Indian comes back?"

"He won't."

"But if he does?"

"We'll kill him, too," Virgil said.

"You don't know what he's like," Mary Beth said.

"No," Virgil said.

He smiled at her.

"But I know what I'm like," Virgil said.

33

Mary Beth and Laurel slept pressed together, with Laurel holding on to Virgil's
sleeve through the night as he slept next to
them. Pony and I took turns staying awake.
At sunup we had coffee and some cold
biscuits, and started north. The women rode
on two of the saddle horses whose owners
we'd killed. We turned the rest of the horses
loose.

"I want my horses," Mary Beth said when
we got her mounted.

"You'll ride a lot more comfortable in a
saddle."

"Can't we put the saddles on my horses?"

"Saddles ain't big enough," Virgil said.
"Horses'll trail along, just like the mule."

And they did. Mary Beth kept looking
back for them every few minutes. Laurel
simply sat on her horse, with the reins
wrapped around the saddle horn. She held
on to the horn, and made no attempt to

direct the horse. If he paused to graze, turned off the trail, Pony or I would ride up and nudge him back. She showed no sign that she was aware of us. She kept her eyes focused on Virgil, who was riding ahead of her with her mother.

At noon we stopped near a stream and let the horses graze on a long tether. There was some shade from a couple of cottonwoods.

"I want to wash myself," Mary Beth said.

"Sure," Virgil said.

"I want to wash myself all over," she said. "Laurel, too."

"We won't look," Virgil said.

"Will you come down and stand close while we go in the water?" Mary Beth said.

"Sure," Virgil said.

He went with them, and when they got to the stream he turned his back. I made fire out of some dead cottonwood branches. Didn't make a good fire. But it would be enough to cook. Pony was slicing salt pork into a fry pan. After I got the fire built I put some biscuits in a Dutch oven and put it next to the fire.

After a time, the women came up from the water, wearing a couple of blankets. Their clothes were draped in the warm wind over the lower branches of one of the cottonwoods. They sat close to Virgil while we ate lunch. By the time we were ready to move on, their clothes were dry enough to wear, and we looked away again while they dressed.

We rode northeast all the rest of the day. Laurel stayed close to her mother, and her mother stayed close to Virgil. As far as they were concerned, it was as if me and Pony were along to carry Virgil's ammunition.

When it was dark, we made camp and sat around the fire with the whiskey jug.

"When we get to Brimstone," Virgil said, "you gonna be able to handle the farm by yourselves?"

"Oh my God," Mary Beth said. "My cow. She has to be milked. What happened to my cow?"

"She's okay," Virgil said. "Got somebody looking after her."

Mary Beth nodded and looked at Laurel. Laurel looked blank. She had a little whiskey in a tin cup and sipped it now and then. Otherwise, she was still. Mary Beth drank some of her whiskey.

"You asked me something," she said to Virgil.

"Can you work the farm by yourself?"

Mary Beth took another swallow of whiskey and let it rest in her mouth for a time before she swallowed.

"I don't know," she said. "I can cook and sew and milk the cow and grow vegetables. I don't know about plowing and digging and hauling. My husband always did that."

"Got any money to hire a hand?" I said.

She seemed startled that I was there. She looked at me long enough to say "No." And then looked back at Virgil.

"Maybe Brother Percival would donate somebody," I said to Virgil.

"But we can't be alone," Mary Beth said.

"Maybe we can arrange a hand," I said.

"No," Virgil said. "She means she can't be alone."

"Anywhere," I said.

Mary Beth nodded. Laurel was still.

"Anywhere," Virgil said.

"That makes it a little harder," I said.

I handed the whiskey jug to Pony; he took a pull and passed it on to Mary Beth. She fastidiously wiped the mouth of the jug with the bottom of her skirt, and poured some whiskey into her cup.

"Can't be alone," she said.

154

34

The next day we came to the Paiute, and a day later, riding up the low rise from the river, we saw the Ostermueller farm. The draught horses that had followed us all the way broke into a trot and went past us, heading for the stock shed. We paused. Virgil glanced at the women. As we sat, tears started down Mary Beth's face.

"Want to stop off here?" Virgil said.

Mary Beth shook her head.

Laurel suddenly kicked her horse in the ribs and hung on to the saddle horn as he broke into a gallop. Pony went after her and caught her as her horse, getting no instructions from its rider, slowed to a walk. He caught the bridle and they stopped. Laurel stayed hunched over the saddle horn, her face turned away from the farmhouse. Pony looked back at Virgil. Virgil gestured toward town. Pony shrugged and let go of the harness, and rode beside her as they went toward Brimstone. As soon as we were past the farm, Laurel slowed her horse until Virgil came up.

"The horses," Mary Beth said.

"Everett'll take care of them, for now," Virgil said. "Till we get you settled."

Mary Beth nodded. They kept riding.

The horses were standing blankly in the stock shed. I tethered my horse, gave the draught horses more food than they needed, and filled the drinking trough. One of the horses paused while he was eating and put his head over into the empty stall where the milk cow had stood. He stood for a moment like that. Then he went back to eating. I put some fresh hay on the floor, hooked the stall gates, and rode after the others.

I caught up with them at the edge of town. We rode in before noon, tied the mule and the horses to the rail in front of the sheriff's office, and went in. Virgil put two chairs out for the women. Then he went and sat at the desk. Laurel sat in the chair nearest Virgil. I took my usual chair, and leaned the eight-gauge against the wall next to me. Pony leaned on the wall by the door.

"Here's what we're going to do," Virgil said. "We're going to get you a nice room at the hotel. They . . ."

"No," Mary Beth said. "No. Not alone.

You can't leave us. Don't leave us. He'll come back. He'll come right into town."

Virgil waited. Laurel sat stiff in her chair. Mary Beth started to cry.

"No, please, no . . ." And then the sobbing overcame her and she couldn't talk.

"We won't leave you alone," Virgil said quietly.

She was too committed to crying to stop all at once. But she cried more gently.

"We get you a room," Virgil said, "that looks out on the lobby. One of us, me, Everett, or Pony . . ."

He looked at Pony. Pony nodded.

Virgil continued.

". . . be sitting right there in the lobby."

"He'll sneak in on us. He'll come in while we're sleeping," Mary Beth said.

"Be on the second floor," Virgil said. "You keep your window locked. And we'll give you a bell."

"Bell?"

"Cowbell," Virgil said. "He ain't gonna know what room you're in. If he does, he ain't gonna climb up the side of the wall. If he could, he'd have to break the window and you'd hear him and ring the bell and we come running."

"What if he kills you?"

"We been doing this kind of work for a

157

long time," Virgil said. "Nobody's killed us yet."

Mary Beth was shaking her head.

"Won't be for long, just while we arrange something for you," Virgil said. "I'll have my . . . I'll have a woman I know come in and see to you. Bring you clothes, things like that. She been through some of what you been through."

"She has? Can she be alone?"

Virgil and I looked at each other.

"She's managing it," Virgil said.

"Well, I can't manage it," she said. "And neither can Laurel."

"Mary Beth," I said. "No such thing as perfect safety. You are as safe now as you have ever been in your life. Or ever will be."

Mary Beth looked at her daughter. Laurel was stiff, and her body was all angles. She registered nothing.

"Lady," Pony said softly from the doorway. "He will not hurt you. I promise he will not."

"What if they don't have a room that you can see the lobby?" she said.

"They will," Virgil said.

Mary Beth had stopped crying.

"This is as safe as I'm ever going to be," she said.

"Or ever were," I said.

"What Everett means," Virgil said, "is safe is more how you feel than how things are. You're safe. You just don't feel it."

Mary Beth nodded.

"Two weeks ago," I said, "you felt safe in your house. And you weren't. Now you don't feel safe with us. And you are."

"Safe and not safe is mostly in your head," Virgil said.

He stood and put out one hand each to Mary Beth and Laurel. Mary Beth took it. Laurel didn't. Virgil didn't seem to notice, except that I knew he did, because Virgil notices everything.

"Here we go," Virgil said.

The women hesitated.

"Bring the eight-gauge," Virgil said to me. "Make everyone feel safer."

"Including you?" I said.

Virgil grinned.

" 'Specially me," he said.

The women stood. Mary Beth first, then Laurel. And we went out of the sheriff's office and walked down to the hotel, Laurel holding on to Virgil's left sleeve. The chances of Buffalo Calf coming into town were very small. The chance that he even knew the women weren't in Mexico was very small. But the women were so scared I found myself keeping an eye out. Just in case.

35

"These women need our help," Allie said to Brother Percival.

Mary Beth and Laurel sat in the front row of pews beside Allie, wearing some clothes that Allie had given them. Brother Percival stood in front of the altar rail, facing them in his white robe, with his long blond hair spilling onto his shoulders, and his thick arms folded across his chest.

"He thinks he's Jesus," I whispered.

"No beard," Virgil said.

Pony stood in the back of the church, by the door. Choctaw Brown stood near him. Choctaw and Pony were studying each other. A couple of other deacons stood against the far wall. There was no one else in the church.

"What is your name?" Percival said.

"Mary Beth Ostermueller."

"Tell me your story, Mary Beth," Brother Percival said.

"An Indian killed my husband and took us," Mary Beth said. "He sold us to some men who were taking us to Mexico when Mr. Cole came and saved us."

"All by yourself," I said.

Virgil ignored me. He was looking at Percival.

"What happened to the men?"

"Mr. Cole killed them."

"Wish I coulda seen it," I whispered.

Virgil shrugged.

"Were you despoiled?" Percival said.

"Despoiled?"

"Did these men do things to you."

"Yes."

"What?"

Mary Beth shook her head.

"We can't talk about it," she said.

"And the young lady?" Brother Percival said.

"My daughter, Laurel."

Percival nodded and spoke to her.

"What do you have to say, Laurel?"

Laurel's silence was like a boulder.

"Does she speak?" Percival said.

"Hasn't spoke since this happened to her," Allie said.

"That right?" Percival said to Mary Beth.

"Yessir," Mary Beth said. "And when we passed our farm she tried to ride off."

"Do you know why?" Percival said.

"It's where her father got killed," Mary Beth said. "Figured it was something about that."

"You own that property?" Percival said.

"Yes, sir."

"Can you work it without a man?" Percival said.

"No, sir," Mary Beth said. "We can't even live there."

"They are afraid," Allie said. "After what happened. They are frightened of being alone."

Percival nodded.

"I understand," he said.

"I thought perhaps that they could live in the single woman's dormitory in the church compound," Allie said rapidly. "I been seeing them every day, you know, and I been thinking about it a lot, and I thought maybe the church could work the farm for them. Sort of as a way for them to pay for their keep here."

Percival stood silent for a while, then looked at Virgil.

"Do you have a thought, Deputy?"

"I believe it is your Christian duty," Virgil said.

"Of course," Percival said.

36

Virgil and I sat in two straight chairs tilted back against the wall on the front porch of the sheriff's office.

"Where's Allie?" I said. "Ain't seen her in a while."

Virgil grinned.

"Miss those lunches?" Virgil said.

"God, no," I said. "She ain't doing your shirts no more, either."

"Nope, taking them to the Chinaman again."

"So she's out closing down saloons?" I said.

"She's at the church, mostly," Virgil said. "I think she adopted them two women."

"Mary Beth and Laurel?"

"Yep."

"Laurel talk yet?" I said.

"Allie says no."

"Seen a doctor?"

"Both of them. Nothing wrong with them

but a few bruises."

"He look at their, ah, private parts?" I said.

"Don't know what he looked at, Everett," Virgil said. "Didn't ask."

"Just thought, since they'd been misused . . ."

"Doctor says they are okay," Virgil said.

"So why don't the girl talk?" I said.

"Don't know."

There were some clouds so that the sky was a pretty even gray, and it looked like it could rain in a while. But it was warm, and the weather still was pleasant.

"How 'bout Mary Beth?" I said.

"She's drinking a lot," Virgil said.

"Can't say I blame her."

"Ain't helping the kid," Virgil said.

"Probably not," I said.

"Allie says that the mother told her they can't be mother and daughter no more," Virgil said.

"So you and Allie are talking 'bout things," I said.

"Yep."

"They can't be mother and daughter because of what happened?" I said.

"Allie said that Mary Beth said that she and the kid seen each other do things that no mother and daughter should ever see."

I nodded.

"Wasn't like they had a choice," I said.

Virgil shrugged.

There was a lot of traffic on Arrow Street. Carriages, buckboards, freight wagon, men on horseback. There were a lot of people walking along the boardwalks and going in and out of shops. From the blacksmith shop across the street and around the corner, I could hear the clang of his hammer.

"How they getting on with the Reverend Brother Percival?" I said.

Virgil grunted.

"He has them in for pastural counseling, every day," Virgil said, "whatever that is."

"Pastoral," I said. "Like a pastor."

"Sure," Virgil said.

"Both of them together?"

"Nope, one at a time," Virgil said.

"Must be an interesting time with the kid," I said.

"Who don't talk," Virgil said.

"I don't like Brother Percival," I said.

"Me neither," Virgil said.

"I think he's got something going on we don't know about," I said.

"Me too."

"How come Choctaw's with him and with Pike?" I said.

" 'Cause Percival's got something going on with Pike."

"Pike ought to love him," I said. "Percival's closing down all Pike's competition."

"Maybe that's what they got going on," Virgil said.

"Nice for Pike," I said. "What's Percival get?"

"Maybe money," Virgil said. "Maybe the joy of doing God's work. Maybe both."

"Thing wrong with folks like the holy Brother Percival," I said, "is that they think they got a right to do anything. Because they doing God's work."

Virgil let his chair tip forward a little and then bumped it back against the wall. He was so balanced, so exact in all his movements, that I figured he could probably balance in that chair if there wasn't any wall.

"Kinda like to know what he's telling those ladies in them pastoral sessions," Virgil said.

"Probably telling 'em they're going to hell," Virgil said.

"For getting raped?" I said.

"Maybe Percival don't see it that way," Virgil said.

"No, maybe he don't," I said.

"Bet God would let that go," Virgil said.

"Yeah, but you don't know," I said. "Percival knows."

"Sure," Virgil said. "Sure he does."

37

I was upstairs in Pike's Palace, lying on a bed with a whore named Frisco. I never knew the rest of her name. But she was a nice girl, except for being a whore. She was clean, and sort of smart, and sort of pretty, and fun to talk to. When I could I'd been keeping company with her since I got to Brimstone.

"Chasing that Indian around didn't wear you down none," Frisco said.

"I'm a lively fella," I said.

"Yes, you are," she said. "I hear those women ain't doing so well."

"They had a rough time," I said.

Frisco grinned.

"Fucking a bunch of men?" she said. "Hell, I do that pretty much every day."

"One of them is fifteen," I said.

"How old you think I was when I started?" Frisco said.

"Soon as you could," I said.

"I wasn't so willing the first few times, either," she said.

"Hard to imagine," I said.

"Well, it's true, and I got over it. Didn't turn into a drunk. Didn't stop talking."

"How you know so much about these women?" I said.

"Whores know a lot," she said.

"You surely do," I said.

"I mean we know a lot about what's going on, lotta men visit with us. Lot of 'em get kind of drunk and kind of excited and they talk about things."

"Why do they get excited?"

"You know damn well why," Frisco said. "Some of the holy church deacons stop by."

"No," I said.

"They ain't as holy as you might think," Frisco said.

"Ain't it a shame," I said.

"Anyway, they tell me that Virgil Cole's woman friend is taking a special interest in them."

"Allie," I said.

"Yep, and that even His Holiness the Reverend Brother Bullshit is talking to them."

"So I hear," I said.

"You like her?" Frisco said.

"Allie?"

"Yes."

"Allie ain't someone you just like or don't like," I said. "You kinda do both."

"Virgil feel that way?"

"He probably likes her more than he don't like her," I said.

"I hear she's had a little something with Brother Bullshit," Frisco said.

"Percival?" I said.

"While you and Virgil was off after that Indian."

"How do you know?"

Frisco smiled.

"I told you, whores know stuff."

"You know if it's true?" I said.

"No," Frisco said. "Not really. Just heard it said."

"Let us agree on something right now," I said.

"I won't say nothing to Virgil," she said.

"Or anybody else," I said.

"Promise."

"I like you, Frisco," I said. "I think you got a good heart. But you spread this story and I will hurt you."

"I promised, Everett. What else you want?"

"I want you to know I'm serious," I said.

"I know that, Everett. I know you're serious."

We lay on the bed for a bit, staring up at

the ceiling of the narrow room. The window was open and the curtains stirred. Frisco sat half up and looked at me.

"Probably ain't so, anyway," she said.

"Probably not," I said.

"Probably just a rumor," Frisco said.

"Long as Virgil don't hear it," I said.

She was silent for another minute, looking at me.

"It always amazes me," she said. "You got all them scars and you ain't dead."

"Sort of amazes me, too," I said.

"Oh, look," she said. "I see a sure sign of life right now."

"Let's not waste it," I said.

38

We were sitting in our chairs in front of the sheriff's office. The day was bright and not hot. The wind moved a little dust around on Arrow Street. We were drinking coffee.

"Big Bend Saloon closed," I said.

"I know," Virgil said.

"Last one," I said.

" 'Cept for Pike's Palace," Virgil said.

"Nice for Pike," I said.

" 'Less Percival closes him down," Virgil said.

"Think that'll happen?" I said.

"Percival's getting to be a pretty grand fella in town," Virgil said.

"I hear people want him to run for councilman," I said.

"Uh-huh."

"On the other hand, there's something going on between Pike and Percival," I said.

"Uh-huh."

Virgil was looking down Arrow Street. A

man in a gray vest and striped pants was walking toward us.

"He shot my horse," he said, when he got close enough.

"Who shot your horse?" Virgil said.

"The Indian."

"Which Indian," Virgil said.

"Big one, black coat and hat," the man said. "Shot my horse right out from under me."

"How come he didn't shoot you?"

"Don't know," the man said. "Sat on his horse ten feet away and looked at me, then he took an arrow out of his boot and tossed it on the ground and rode off."

"You armed?" Virgil said.

"No."

"Where'd it happen?"

"Right outside town, just past the ford."

"What's your name?" Virgil said.

"Stroud."

"Okay, Mr. Stroud," Virgil said. "We'll take a look."

"I liked that horse," Stroud said.

"See what we can do," Virgil said. "Everett, try to find Pony."

I took the eight-gauge and headed for Pike's Palace.

An hour later the three of us were sitting on our horses, looking at Stroud's dead

173

horse. Pony climbed down and picked up the arrow that lay on the ground near the horse. He looked at it for a moment and handed it to Virgil.

"Same thing," Virgil said, and handed it to me.

"No arrowhead," I said.

Pony circled the dead horse in steadily widening circles. Twenty feet from the horse, he stopped and sat on his heels and studied the ground.

Then he pointed south, along the river.

"Gone this way," Pony said. "Come this way same."

"Okay," Virgil said.

We rode south along the river. The hoof-prints were plain enough. I could have followed them, too.

"Going fast," Pony said after a while.

I could see that the prints were deeper and farther apart, with a little rim of dirt pushed up in back of each print.

"Why you suppose he didn't kill that fella?" Virgil said.

"Stroud?" I said. "I'm guessing he wanted us to hear about it quick."

"So we'd come out looking for him quick," Virgil said.

"Maybe," I said. "Why would he be in a hurry?"

"Mighta been a day, maybe longer, 'fore someone found the dead man and told us," Virgil said.

We rode in silence, following Pony as he tracked.

"Probably took Stroud an hour to walk in from where his horse got shot," Virgil said. "And it took us maybe another hour to find Pony and saddle up and get out here and look around."

"So, say he's got two hours on us," I said.

"And he's pushing his horse," Virgil said.

"Can't push him forever," I said.

"Unless he got more than one," Virgil said. "And even if he don't, he can widen the gap between us."

"So he isn't trying to walk us into an ambush," I said.

"Don't seem so," Virgil said. "He was doing that, he'd want us to catch up."

"He wants us out of town," I said.

"Seems so," Virgil said.

"We could head back to town now," I said.

"Yep."

"But if we're wrong," I said, "we lose the chance to catch him."

"Yep."

Pony turned to the riverbank, which was probably twenty feet high at this point.

"Jefe," Pony said.

175

Virgil and I moved up beside him. Pony pointed at the horse tracks.

"Into the river," Pony said.

"From here?" I said.

Pony pointed again.

"Horse go down," he said.

We looked at the gouges and drag marks in the riverbank.

"Why not wait for the ford," I said, "downriver?"

"It's what he's hoping we'll do," Virgil said.

Pony patted his horse's neck.

"We go down," Pony said, and kicked the horse toward the bank. The horse balked. Pony kicked him again, leaning over the horse's neck. He was speaking to him in Apache, too fast and soft for me to make any of it out. The horse went over the edge, front legs stiff out ahead of him, back legs bunched, and began to slide and scramble down the near-vertical slope, with Pony crouched up over his neck. Pony let the reins drape over the saddle horn and held on to the horse's mane, still talking to him in Apache.

And then they were down and into the river. It was deep here, so the horse had to swim. Pony slid out of the saddle as they went in and they swam together, with

Pony's hand on the saddle horn to the other side. When they reached the other side, I saw why the Indian had gone in here. There was a short strip of dry land at the foot of the far bank, and a narrow arroyo, cut by spring rains, that Pony was able to lead his horse into. We lost sight of them for a little while, and then they appeared at the top of the bank on the other side.

"That would have been the place for the ambush," I said.

Virgil nodded.

Holding his horse's reins, Pony crouched again and looked at the sign. Then he swung up into his wet saddle and pointed north, back the way we'd come, and began to follow the tracks.

I looked at the riverbank.

"Nothing says we have to go across here," I said.

"Nope," Virgil said. "But I'm thinking that one of the reasons he went across is if you went after him, you couldn't get back."

"So you'd get back to town at least two hours after he did," I said. "No shortcuts."

"Yep."

"But," I said, "we ain't over there, and if we head straight northeast, and don't stay with the river, we can probably close that by an hour."

"And if we ain't got it figured right," Virgil said, "we're leaving Pony to go up against this fella by himself."

"Pony ain't no bank clerk," I said. " 'Sides, what would we do for him over here."

"You're thinking 'bout the eight-gauge," Virgil said. "With a Winchester I could hit a jackrabbit from here, never mind a big Indian in a black coat."

"So, which is it?" I said. "The town, or Pony?"

"We get back to town quick as we can, we're still an hour after him," Virgil said.

"And it don't figure that whatever he's doing, he'll spend an hour doing it," I said.

Virgil nodded.

"So, it's Pony," I said.

"It is," Virgil said.

"Good," I said.

We rode north along the river, with Pony on the other side. At the ford near town, Pony stopped beside a riderless horse. The horse wore no saddle or bridle. Pony got down and looked at his hooves. Then he looked at the ground for a moment and got back up on his horse. He came across the river.

"Other horse," he said.

"Hid him near the ford," Virgil said.

Pony was looking at the ground.

"Ride him to town," Pony said.

"So he's got a fresh mount," I said.

Virgil nodded.

"Let's see what he did," Virgil said.

And we rode into town, following the fresh tracks of the new horse straight down Arrow Street.

39

There were a lot of people standing around on Arrow Street as we rode into town. There was a crowd in front of Pike's Palace, looking at the shattered front windows in the swinging doors.

Pike came out of the saloon and stood on the porch.

"Pony," he said. "Where the fuck were you?"

Pony grinned and made a big circular motion with his hand.

"Round and round," he said.

"And you fucking deputies," Pike said. "Where the fuck you been?"

With no expression on his face, Virgil looked at Pike for a long silent moment.

Then he said, "Round and round."

"Fucking Indian rode in here, dozen people saw him, big as life," Pike said. "Like he's the fucking mayor or something. Rides right up Arrow Street. Hauls out a shotgun and unloads both barrels through my windows. You know how much those cocksuckers cost me? They come all the way from fucking Saint Louis, and that fucking red nigger blows them apart and rides out."

"Anybody hurt?" I said.

"Couple of drunks got nicked," Pike said. "They'll live."

Virgil was looking at the street in front of the saloon.

"Left him an arrow," Virgil said.

I nodded.

"I don't give a fuck what he left. What are you gonna do about it."

"We'll probably chase him again," Virgil said.

"Don't bother," Pike said. "I sent Kirby and J.D. after him."

"Anybody else?" Virgil said.

"J.D. and Kirby's usually enough," Pike said.

Virgil nodded.

"You know why this fella shot up your saloon," he said.

" 'Cause he's a fucking prairie coon, and he don't know what else to do," Pike said.

Virgil nodded.

"Figured there'd be a reason," he said. "Pony, come on down to the office with us."

"I want Pony here," Pike said.

"None of us cares much what you want, at this here moment," Virgil said. "Me and Everett are deputy sheriffs, and we're planning to question Pony."

Pike looked at Virgil. Virgil looked back. The crowd began to open up a little. I stepped away from Virgil and rested the eight-gauge barrel up on my shoulder, and thumbed both hammers back. It was so quiet that I could hear the sound of cicadas singing.

They sang for a while.

Then Pike said, "Pony, when you're through with the deputies, come on back here, if you would."

Pony nodded, and turned and walked down to the office with me and Virgil. Behind us, Pike went back into his saloon, and the crowd began to thin out.

40

"Whaddya think?" Virgil said to Pony as we sat out front of the sheriff's office and looked at things.

"J.D. and Kirby town men," Pony said. "Good with guns, but . . ." He shook his head.

"Not so good on the prairie?" Virgil said.

"No," Pony said.

"Not as good as the Indian," Virgil said.

"No."

"You as good as the Indian?" Virgil said.

Pony nodded.

"Better," he said.

The stage from Barrow went past, heading for the St. Louis Hotel, the big draft horses walking easily. The driver held the reins loosely. They'd made the run so often that the horses knew when to slow down and where to go.

"This whole thing was supposed to get someone to ride out after the Indian," I said.

"Seems so," Virgil said.

"He didn't go to all this trouble to get us out of town so he could ride in and shoot out Pike's windows," I said.

"Think he wanted J.D. and Kirby?" Virgil said.

"I think he wanted Pike," I said.

"Makes more sense," Virgil said. "Don't it."

"Certainly gotta be some reason he's hanging around here," I said. " 'Stead of someplace else."

"Same reason," Pony said, "coyotes around dead buffalo."

"Just that?" I said. " 'Cause the killing is easy?"

Pony shrugged.

"Maybe," he said.

"Any reason he might have for killing people round here?" Virgil said.

"Indian people always have reason to kill white people," Pony said.

Virgil nodded.

"Indian always happy to kill white," Pony said. "So this Indian come here and he kill cow and not much happen. Except he get some beef. Then he kill a man and steal his horses. He get to do something he like, and he get to take horses, and he get to look at you."

"Us," Virgil said.

"Yes, he get to see what you are like."

"Same with the women?"

Pony nodded.

"Kill white man, take white women, have white women, sell white women, see what you do."

"And now this," Virgil said.

Pony nodded again.

"You think it's about Pike?" Virgil said.

"Maybe," Pony said. "Maybe about you."

Virgil was sitting with his chair tilted back. He let it slowly come forward until it was flat.

"He's thinking we'll come after him," Virgil said.

"Maybe," Pony said.

"So maybe it ain't about Pike," Virgil said.

"Maybe about all," Pony said.

"Pike and Everett and me."

"Might," Pony said.

"You been with Pike a long time," Virgil said.

"Scouted for him in Army," Pony said.

"He done anything," Virgil said, "you know about, might rile this Indian?"

"Pike killed a lot of Indians," Pony said.

"But you work for him," I said.

"Half Mexican," Pony said.

"And half Indian," I said.

185

"Half Chiricahua," Pony said. "Pike didn't kill no Chiricahua."

"Who'd he kill most?" Virgil said.

"Comanche," Pony said. "Hell, I kill Comanche, too."

"Think this Indian's Comanche?" Virgil said.

"Don't know," Pony said. "It's Comanche land. Arrow could be Comanche."

"But you don't know," I said.

"Indian make arrow out of what he can find," Pony said. " 'Specially toy arrow he going to leave behind."

"Name's Buffalo Calf," I said.

Pony shrugged.

"Speaks English good," Virgil said.

"Me too," Pony said.

"Sometimes," I said, "some Indians' camp would get wiped out and they'd take a couple kids that survived and send them to Indian school. Teach them to be good Americans."

Virgil nodded. He sat silently for a while, then tilted his chair back again and looked at the street.

"So maybe he's after Pike because Pike killed some Comanches when he was in the Army," Virgil said.

"Not in battle, though," I said. "Comanches see death in battle as honorable. Part

186

of how things are. No reason to revenge such a death."

"So it would be something else, then," Virgil said.

"Maybe women, children, something like that," I said.

"Pony?" Virgil said.

"Sí, jefe," Pony said. "Comanche people, Chiricahua people, most Indian people, death between warriors *honrosco*."

"And maybe Buffalo Calf got scooped up and sent to school," Virgil said. "And now he's grown up and wants revenge?"

Pony shrugged. I shrugged.

"Could be," I said.

"So, if he's after Pike, why all the rigmarole," Virgil said.

"Maybe he wants Pike to know it's him," I said. "And to think about it. Maybe it's got some private meaning to him."

"And maybe we got it all wrong," Virgil said.

"And maybe we'll never know, even when it's over," I said.

"Sometimes you don't," Virgil said.

"Even if you went to West Point?" I said.

"Maybe even then," Virgil said.

"Disappointing," I said.

"Sometimes it's just about shooting," Virgil said.

"Least we're good at that," I said.

"And if it ain't Pike?" Virgil said. "Why us?"

"Power?" I said, and looked at Pony.

Pony nodded.

"He see you come look at first dead man," Pony said. "He see you come take women back. See you have power. He kill you. He take your power."

"And Pike?" Virgil said.

"He kills Pike," I said, "we still have power."

Virgil nodded.

"Complexicated," he said.

"Very," I said.

Virgil looked at Pony, who was looking at nothing and seeing everything, the way Virgil did.

"Maybe J.D. and Kirby will get him," Virgil said.

Pony shook his head.

"You with us on this?" Virgil said. "If they don't?"

"Yes," Pony said.

Virgil grinned at him.

"You after his power?" Virgil said.

Pony didn't grin, but he looked like he might have.

"Sí, jefe," he said.

41

Mary Beth came into the sheriff's office after lunchtime, mush-mouth drunk and weaving as she walked.

"Wanna report a man fuckin' a child," she mumbled.

Virgil stood and went around his desk and eased her onto a chair. Then he sat on the edge of his desk right in front of her.

"A man fucking a child," Virgil said.

"Used to fuck me, now he fuckin' her."

Virgil nodded.

"You thinking about what happened to you and Laurel, 'fore we found you?"

"Naw," Mary Beth said. "Brother Percival fucking us."

"You let him?" Virgil said.

"I don' . . ."

Mary Beth slid suddenly off the chair. Quick as he was, Virgil got a hold of her as she went and broke her fall. He eased her the rest of the way down and she sat on the floor with her legs splayed.

"Everett," Virgil said. "Whyn't you go see if you can find Allie."

I nodded and left.

I found her in The Church of the Brotherhood, practicing on the organ. To me it sounded like a cow in labor, but I was never musical.

"What's wrong?" she said when she saw me.

"Nothing bad," I said. "Mary Beth Ostermueller is drunk and falling down in Virgil's office."

Allie stood up.

"Oh, God," she said.

As we walked down to the office, Allie said, "What is she doing there. What is she telling you?"

"She was telling us that Brother Percival was fucking Laurel," I said. " 'Fore she fell off the chair and Virgil caught her."

"That's ridiculous," Allie said.

"Said he'd been doing it to both of them," I said.

"Brother Percival is a man of God."

"I've heard even they do it, sometimes," I said.

"Not if they are holy men like Brother Percival," Allie said.

"He ever show any interest in you?" I said.

"Of course he shows interest. He cares about my soul. He shows interest in everyone."

"Care about any of your other parts?" I said.

"Everett!"

When we were at the office, I opened the door and ushered her in. Virgil was at his desk, his feet up, his white shirt gleaming from the laundry.

"Where's Mary Beth?" Allie said.

"Sleeping in a cell," Virgil said.

"What did she tell you?" Allie said.

"Not much," Virgil said.

"Everett says she's been accusing Brother Percival."

"She said he was poking Laurel," Virgil said.

"Everett says she was drunk."

"Seemed so," Virgil said.

"She's drunk all the time," Allie said.

"Don't mean she's lying," Virgil said.

"Not on purpose," Allie said. "I know that she had a bad time when the Indian took her. Laurel, too. And it made her crazy, and when she's drunk she's crazier. I been trying to help her, and help Laurel, and so has Brother Percival."

"Girl talking yet?" Virgil said.

191

"No," Allie said. "And Mary Beth's crawled into her bottle and given up being a mother."

"So who looks out for the daughter?" Virgil said.

"I do. I've become the closest thing she has to a mother."

"And she ain't, ah, indicated nothing to you about Brother Percival's intentions."

"No, of course not. You think I would stand by and let that happen? She's like a daughter to me."

Virgil nodded. I poured myself a cup of coffee.

"Well," Virgil said. "Me and Everett are deputy sheriffs here. I guess we got to go talk with Brother Percy."

"He doesn't like to be called Percy," Allie said.

Virgil nodded.

"I'll keep it in mind," he said. "You mind sticking here and looking after her if she wakes up?"

"I've done it before," Allie said.

"Good," Virgil said. " 'Preciate it."

"And you're really going to talk with Brother Percival?" Allie said.

"Just doing my duty," Virgil said.

"She'll say anything," Allie said.

"I know," Virgil said.

"You can't believe anything she says."

"I know."

"She didn't tell you anything about me?" Allie said.

"Anything to tell?" Virgil said.

"Virgil, you shouldn't ask me a thing like that," Allie said. "Of course there isn't anything. What do you think I am?"

"Just asking," Virgil said.

"You know how drunks are," Allie said. "They don't remember things that happened. They remember things that didn't happen. They make up stories. They'll say anything."

"Keep that in mind, too," Virgil said.

He stood. I put down my coffee cup, and we went out into the street.

"Mary Beth tell you anything you haven't mentioned?" I said to Virgil as we walked toward the church.

Virgil didn't answer. When Virgil doesn't answer, it isn't because he didn't hear the question.

I didn't press it.

42

We talked to Brother Percival in the front room of his house in the compound in back of the church.

"Where's my organist?" Brother Percival said, and smiled.

He was in his official church clothes: white robe, sandals, long hair.

"Allie's looking out for a drunk down at the jail," Virgil said. "Woman named Mary Beth Ostermueller."

"Poor Mary Beth," Percival said. "We're all trying to help her, but . . ."

"She says you're fucking her daughter," Virgil said.

Percival looked like he might burst into prayer.

"Oh, dear Lord," he said.

"Said you was fucking her, and now you're fucking Laurel."

"Must you speak so coarsely, Deputy?" Percival said.

"Just quoting Mary Beth, Reverend," Virgil said.

"She was drunk."

"She was."

"The charge is, as you must know, entirely untrue," Brother Percival said.

The front room of Brother Percival's house wasn't much: a table and chair, an uncomfortable-looking round-backed blue couch, a large Bible on a stand near the door. A big photograph of Brother Percival hung in an oval frame on the wall. In the picture he was wearing a dark suit with a vest and a white shirt with a dark tie. In the picture, his hair was short.

"I'm sure it is, Reverend," Virgil said. "But me 'n Everett, here, bein' law officers, we have to ask."

"Of course you do," Percival said. "I understand perfectly."

"Got any idea why she might be thinking these things about you?" Virgil said.

"Aside from drunkenness?" Percival said.

" 'Side from that," Virgil said.

"Perhaps my attempts to share my religion with them, to help them, somehow became distorted in her degenerated mind. What happened to her and all. The poor woman clearly isn't right."

"Something's wrong," Virgil said. "Tell me

195

a little 'bout your religion."

"My religion is the presence of God in me."

"How's God feel about sex?" Virgil said.

"Do not blaspheme," Percival said.

"Sorry," Virgil said. "Tell me a little 'bout how you been trying to help these two ladies we brought you."

"I counsel them every day," Percival said.

"Meanin' you take them someplace and talk to them," Virgil said.

"Yes," Percival said. "I talk with them here. Though it is, of course, a bit more than that."

"Girl talk any?"

"Not yet," Percival said. "Poor child."

"Well, she probably don't argue much," Virgil said.

"No, she surely doesn't," Percival said. "I'm not sure she understands what I'm saying. I'm not sure she is at all in her right mind."

"What are you saying?" I said.

"I explain to them that His eye is on the fall of a sparrow," Percival said. "That He never sends you a burden too great for you to bear."

"Ain't found that to be the case myself, Reverend," Virgil said. "But you probably know more than I do 'bout all that."

"I know that the Lord resides in me," Percival said. "I know what the Lord shares with me."

"Lord always been there?" Virgil said.

"He is always there in all of us," Percival said. "But many of us deny him."

He looked sort of pointedly, I thought, at me and Virgil.

"Didn't realize he was there," I said.

"I denied him, at first," Percival said. "There was a time when I denied God, when I lived a life of the physical self, when I drank, when I committed fornication, when I relied on violence. But God would not be denied. He battered my defenses. He forced himself upon me until we have become one."

"You and God?" I said.

"Yes."

"One thing?" I said.

"Yes."

"You and God being one thing," I said. "Must be pretty hard to think anything you do is wrong."

"The Lord governs me in all things," Percival said.

"He tell you to keep Choctaw Brown on the payroll?" Virgil said.

"As you must know, there is no payroll," Percival said. "Choctaw came to me, as I had been. He came from a life of dissipation and cruelty. He said he wanted to be saved. We welcomed him to the brotherhood."

"He saved?" I said.

"He is."

"Still wearing a Colt," Virgil said.

"I told you we are militant Christians," Percival said. "We will not allow those who have not been saved to do us harm."

"I guess probably I ain't been saved yet," Virgil said. "But I don't want you touching that girl."

"To accuse me is to accuse the Lord, who abides in me."

"Seems to be the case," Virgil said.

Percival seemed to get taller as he stood in front of us. He folded his big arms across his wide chest.

"You can't accuse me," Percival said.

His voice was firm but not very loud.

"Because of the Lord?" I said.

"We are one," Percival said. "You cannot accuse us."

Virgil looked at Percival for a while, the way you'd look at an odd insect you'd found. Percival stood with his arms still folded like he was going to give the Sermon on the Mount. Then he turned and stalked out of the room.

As we walked back to the sheriff's office, Virgil said, "You believe any of that?"

"Sure," I said. "Like I believe the world's flat."

"Looks flat," Virgil said.

"But it ain't."

"Can't prove it ain't," Virgil said.

"You believe what Percival's saying?"

Virgil shook his head.

"I think he'd fuck a snake if you held it for him," Virgil said.

"You think he believes what he's saying?" I said.

"He might," Virgil said.

"Think he's been bothering the women?" I said.

"Something you mentioned," Virgil said. "You mentioned that if he thought God was in him and he was, you know, part of God, and God was part of him, then he'd feel pretty good about doing anything he wanted."

"Anything God does is the right thing to do," I said.

"You think he thinks he's God?"

"Might," I said.

"That's disappointing," Virgil said.

" 'Cause you thought you were?"

"Still do," Virgil said. "Just don't like it that Percival thinks different."

199

"So we know it," I said.

"Can't prove it," Virgil said.

"Mary Beth saying so ain't enough?"

"Nope," Virgil said. "Too drunk."

"We could shoot him anyway, just to be safe," I said.

"Can't do that," Virgil said. "Got to know."

"How you gonna know?" I said.

"Gotta ask the girl," he said.

43

Allie brought Laurel down to the office.

"She got anything to say about Percival," Virgil said, "better to ask her here."

Allie sat with Laurel on the couch. I leaned on the doorjamb. Virgil moved his chair to the couch and sat down in front of Laurel.

"You remember me, Virgil," he said.

She might have nodded.

"I need to ask you some questions about Brother Percival. And I need you to tell me the answers."

She stared at him as if he hadn't spoken.

"I can whisper to you," Virgil said. "And you can whisper back to me if you want to, but I need you to help me with this."

"Go ahead, honey," Allie said. "You can do it. It's important."

Laurel showed no sign that she heard.

Virgil sat quietly for a time. No one can be as quiet as Virgil Cole, when he wanted to be quiet.

After a little time, he said, "Allie, you and Everett wait outside."

Allie looked at Laurel.

"You all right with that, honey," she said.

"We'll be okay," Virgil said.

Again, Laurel might have nodded. I opened the office door and stood aside. Allie didn't seem pleased. But she stood and went out. I followed her and closed the door. We stood near the front window and watched. Virgil took off his hat and put it on the desk behind him. Then he leaned forward and put his face next to Laurel's and whispered something. He waited. She was motionless. He leaned forward again and whispered and then put his ear next to her lips. The two of them sat that way, with their heads together, Virgil's hands folded in his lap. I could see that he was whispering.

"What is he doing?" Allie said.

"Whispering," I said.

"I don't know if she should be left alone with a man after what happened to her," Allie said.

"Don't seem to mind," I said.

"And Virgil did rescue her," Allie said.

"All by himself," I said.

"No, you know what I mean."

202

"Virgil was in charge," I said.

"Virgil's always in charge," Allie said.

"True," I said.

"How's he know to whisper to her?" Allie said.

"Virgil knows things," I said.

"How's he know it's the right thing to do?"

"Virgil always knows what he's doing is the right thing to do," I said. " 'Cept when it ain't, and he knows that, too."

"I guess I still don't understand him," Allie said.

"Nothing to understand," I said. "Virgil don't never pretend."

We watched the whispered pantomime through the office window. Laurel was still motionless, her head and Virgil's close together. I couldn't tell if she was making any response. But she hadn't pulled away. I realized that while their heads were close together, Virgil was not touching Laurel.

"I don't know anyone like him," Allie said. "Do you?"

"You don't get to be Virgil Cole," I said, "being like other folks."

In the office I saw Virgil nod his head. Then Laurel nodded hers. They still had their heads close to each other.

"Jesus," I said. "I think they're talking."

"My God," Allie said.

Virgil nodded again. And waited. And nodded again. And whispered. Laurel nodded. Virgil nodded slowly and kept it up, as if Laurel was saying things he agreed with. Then she leaned forward and put her face against his neck and cried. Virgil sat quietly. He didn't make any move to touch her.

"I better get in there," Allie said.

"No," I said.

"She's crying," Allie said.

I blocked the doorway.

"No," I said.

She couldn't get by me, and she knew it. So we turned back to the window. Inside, Virgil sat quietly while Laurel cried. After a time she stopped and raised her head and sat back. Virgil sat back, too. He reached behind him to the desk and picked up his hat. He put it on and adjusted it, and nodded once at Laurel.

She smiled at him.

"Did she smile?" Allie said.

"Yes," I said.

He stood and came to the door and opened it.

"We're done in here," Virgil said.

"She spoke?" Allie said.

"Yes."

"What did she say?" Allie said.

"I promised I wouldn't tell," Virgil said.

Allie looked like she wanted to argue, but she didn't. Laurel stood.

Virgil said, "I'll come by. We'll take a walk."

Laurel nodded.

"Maybe tomorrow," Virgil said.

Laurel nodded.

He looked at Allie.

"Stay with her," he said.

"I will," Allie said. "I do."

She put her arm around Laurel and they went out of the office.

I looked at Virgil. He shrugged slightly. I didn't ask him what she'd said. I knew he wouldn't tell me.

44

Two saddle horses plodded up Arrow Street, each dragging something. Sitting on the front porch, Virgil and I watched them come. As they got closer we could see that what they were dragging were the bodies of two men.

I stood.

Virgil said, "Let's see where they're going."

We went out to the street as the horses passed and followed them up Arrow Street. The dead men were covered with dirt, and their heads were black with dried blood.

"Scalped," Virgil said.

I nodded.

"You recognize them?" I said.

"Kinda hard, them being such a mess," Virgil said.

"Want to guess?" I said.

"J.D. and Kirby," Virgil said.

"What I'm guessing," I said.

At Fifth Street, the horses stopped in front of Pike's Palace and stood at the hitching rail, and drank from the trough. Virgil went and looked at one of the dead men.

"J.D.," he said.

He looked at the second man.

"Kirby," he said.

"They were good," I said.

"Not as good as the Indian," Virgil said.

"Guess the Indian's got their power," I said.

"Guess," Virgil said.

"No arrow," I said. "Probably figured it would fall out while they were dragging into town."

"Scalping sends the same message," Virgil said.

"Don't look like they been dragged far," I said.

"I'd guess edge of town," Virgil said.

"So he kills them," I said, "brings them to the edge of town, hitches them up, and lets the horses drag 'em in."

"Knows they'll head for home."

"Which they did," I said.

Virgil nodded.

"So Pike'd see them," Virgil said.

"And we would, too," I said.

Virgil nodded again, looking at the dead men.

"They're too dirty to make out how he killed them," I said.

Virgil continued to nod.

"Guess we got to go get him," Virgil said.

"Yep."

"Got stuff to do in town," Virgil said.

"I know."

Virgil stared at the dead men.

"Got to go get him," he said again.

Pike came out of the front door of the Palace and looked down at the dead men. Pony came out behind him.

"That fucking Indian," he said.

"Which one?" Virgil said.

"Buffalo Calf," Pike said.

"You know it's him?" Virgil said.

"I know it's him," Pike said. "It's always him, the fuck."

"Always?" Virgil said.

"I know it's him," Pike said. "And I'm through with it. I'm going after him."

"We'll do that," Virgil said.

"The hell you will," Pike said. "The fucker didn't kill two of your people."

"We'll go after him," Virgil said.

"You can go with me, you want to," Pike said, "or not, but I'm riding out of here in an hour with twenty men. And we're going to bring him back in pieces. Nobody does that to me."

208

"Do what you gotta do," Virgil said. "Me and Everett are gonna need Pony."

"Pony goes with me," Pike said.

Virgil looked at Pony.

"I go with Virgil and Everett," Pony said.

"You work for me, you half-breed cocksucker," Pike said.

"No more," Pony said.

"Fuck you, then," Pike said. "I'll track him myself."

He turned and walked back into the Palace.

"Pike ain't his usual jolly self," I said.

"Twenty men," Pony said. "Stampede. Be lucky he don't kill them all."

Virgil nodded, looking at the empty doorway where Pike had gone.

"Be lucky," Virgil said.

45

We sat our horses on the other side of the ford and looked at the muddle of hoofprints that Pike and his posse had left. The pack mule took the opportunity to graze.

"Don't make tracking the Indian so easy," Virgil said.

"I find him," Pony said.

"Pike will assume he's running," I said.

"Not running," Pony said.

"He'll shadow Pike," Virgil said.

"If we're right about him," I said.

"So, we shadow Pike, we might come across him."

"Might shadow us," Pony said.

"He and Pike got a history," Virgil said. "I ain't saying he got no interest in us. But they got something between them."

"Maybe get everybody," Pony said.

"Might be his plan," I said.

Virgil was looking at the tracks of twenty horses.

"Pike much of an Indian fighter, when you was with him?"

"Very good soldier," Pony said. "Kill everybody."

"And if Buffalo Calf wants to be tracked, Pike won't have much trouble."

"No track like me," Pony said. "But can track. I teach him."

"When you was soldiering, Everett, what you do with a troop of soldiers like this?"

"They'd be in squads," I said. "Non com for each. I'd have scouts ahead, maybe some outriders to each flank."

"Let's follow along, see if he does that."

"Think you can track them, Pony?"

"Little girl we save?" Pony said. "She could track them."

"If we're right," Virgil said, "the Indian's trying to lead Pike into a trap. Be better if we didn't ride right into it behind them."

"They rode out at sunup," I said.

Virgil glanced at the sun.

"Got 'bout two hours on us," he said.

He looked at the horizon in all directions.

"Land's flat for a ways," he said. "Don't see no place he could hide and watch."

"So Buffalo Calf has got to trust Pike to follow him," I said, "until they get into country where Buffalo Calf can spy."

"You know this country, Pony?" Virgil said.

"Some," Pony said. "Northwest, maybe two days' ride, country get rougher."

"That where you'd go," Virgil said, "you was gonna ambush somebody?"

"Yes," Pony said.

Virgil looked at the sun again.

"We'll follow them," he said. "See if they turn that way."

"And if they do?" I said.

"Maybe strike out on our own," Virgil said.

He clucked to his horse. The mule heard him and pricked his ears forward and stopped grazing. We rode out after Pike, and the mule trotted on behind us. We all had .45 Winchesters, in the saddle boot, and we all wore .45 Colts. Made carrying cartridges easier. I had the eight-gauge. We all rode together. The mule could have followed Pike's trail.

About midday we came to the place where they'd stopped and reorganized. We sat our horses while Pony rode around the area, looking at tracks.

"Okay," Pony said. "He send scouts."

He pointed out the tracks of two individual horses.

He rode around the area some more.

"Outriders," he said, pointing.

"Okay," I said. "He's getting organized."

"Good soldier," Pony said. "Know how to fight."

"Probably got them broken into squads now," I said.

"No way to tell," Pony said. "Horses all walk over each other tracks in troop."

"He actually got twenty men?" Virgil said.

"Cannot tell," Pony said. "Too many."

"Let's assume twenty," I said. "He sent two scouts out front, and two flankers. Leaves sixteen. So he breaks the rest of them into three squads of five. And he makes sixteen."

"All he needs is a damned guidon," Virgil said.

"It's the way he's learned to fight," I said.

"There's enough of them to be stupid," Virgil said.

"They figure Buffalo Calf won't turn and fight them?" I said.

"Yep."

"So they could ride right on into an ambush," I said.

"Could," Virgil said

"Maybe Buffalo Calf has some friends," I said.

"None before," Pony said.

"Any Comanche villages around?" Virgil said.

Pony shook his head.

"Mostly reservation Indians now," Pony said.

"Don't mean they always stay on the reservation," Virgil said.

"Nope," Pony said.

"You think he knows we're out here?" I said to Pony.

"Probably think we with Pike," Pony said. "Even mission-school Indian don't understand white people much."

"You understand white people?" I said.

"No," Pony said.

His face was blank. I grinned at him.

"Well," I said. "We ain't typical, anyway."

"Typical?" Pony said.

"Like everybody else," I said.

"No," Pony said. "You not like everybody."

46

We had a cold camp that night, no fire, beef jerky and hard biscuits for supper, some whiskey to wash it down. In the morning, more biscuits and jerky, and some water from the canteen. Not long after sunrise, the tracks turned northwest.

"How far to this high ground you talking about," Virgil said.

"Half day," Pony said. "Less, if push horse."

"Okay," Virgil said. "Take a look, see how far he sends his outriders."

Pony nodded and turned his horse and rode in a widening circle around the main tracks until he found the outriders. We sat our horses and waited.

"Both side," Pony said, when he came back. "Maybe far as you shoot Colt."

Virgil nodded.

"Want to get beyond the outriders," he said.

Pony nodded.

"Tell me 'bout this high ground," Virgil said.

"Start like short hill," Pony said. "Go up."

Pony made a steep gesture with his hand.

"Get to be like short mountain," he said. "Many rocks. Many arroyo."

"It's straight northwest," Virgil said, pointing in the direction the tracks took.

"Sí, jefe."

"So we go straight north awhile," Virgil said, "and turn straight left, we might come in behind the Indian."

Pony nodded.

"What you think, Everett," Virgil said.

"This is a smart Indian," I said.

"We're all smart," Virgil said. "See who's smarter."

We turned north. We weren't tracking now, so we could go hard.

"You know what we're trying to do, Pony," Virgil said. "Tell us when to turn west."

We crossed the outriders' tracks as we rode north, and went several miles beyond them. Then Pony turned his horse west, and we followed. In the late afternoon we saw the high ground in the distance stretching north. The flat land from which it rose was well to our south.

"Pretty good," I said to Pony.

"Sí," he said.

The going became harder as we went up the eastern slope of the hill. It was as Pony had said, full of rock outcroppings, laced with shale-sided arroyos. We went on up with Pony in the lead. He was leaning out of his saddle now, looking at the ground. I took the eight-gauge out of its scabbard and held it across my saddle. It was dark when we reached the top of the rise. There was no moon or stars. If there was anything to look at, it would have to wait until morning. Pony dismounted and walked ahead, leading his horse. We followed him, also leading the animals. In a while we came to the place Pony was looking for. A stream emerged from between two boulders and ran off downhill into the darkness.

"No fire," Virgil said.

We let the animals drink. There wasn't enough forage here, so we fed them some corn from a sack that the mule carried. We fed ourselves more jerky and biscuits. We drank a little whiskey, and decided who would take the first watch. It was Pony. Virgil and I wrapped ourselves in saddle blankets and went to sleep on the ground. About the time Pony woke me for my watch it had begun to rain. We wrapped ourselves in our slickers and hunched against the rock.

47

It was still raining and overcast in the morning, and much cooler than it had been. But in the gray light we could see the flat land to our southeast, and on it, in the distance, Pike's posse. Virgil got a brass telescope from his saddlebag and gazed through it for a while.

"Christ, he brought everybody but the whores," Virgil said.

He handed it to me.

"I count twenty," I said.

Virgil nodded.

"You see the Indian?" he said to Pony.

Pony shook his head.

"This stream the only water around?" Virgil said.

"Yes," Pony said.

"Horse got to drink," Virgil said. "Him, too."

"So if he's camped here," I said, "he's probably beside the stream."

Below us on the plain, Pike's posse set out toward the hills. Virgil watched them for a little while. Then he put down the glass and glanced up at the dark sky and shrugged.

"Take 'em a while," he said. "What's down below."

"Pass down there," Pony said. "Halfway up hill, maybe. All rock. Hoofprints stop in there."

"You think he'll lead them in there?"

"He know Pike," Pony said. "He know Pike not go in there."

"Nobody would go in there," I said.

"What's he do if the trail leads in there, Captain?" Virgil said.

"He splits his troops," I said. "And stays on the high ground, on each side."

"And looks for the ambush," Virgil said.

"Yep."

"Indian know that?" Virgil said to Pony.

"If he ever fight soldiers," Pony said.

"If he leads him in there," Virgil said, "he gets Pike to split his posse, and half of them are on the wrong side of the canyon when the fight starts."

Pony nodded.

"He that smart?" Virgil said.

"Smart Indian," Pony said.

"Can anybody get across the pass?" Virgil said.

"Too wide to jump," Pony said. "Too much straight up to climb."

"So they can't?"

"Nope."

"I figure he wants Pike," Virgil said. "What if Pike's on the wrong side from him?"

"Not too wide for rifle," Pony said.

Virgil nodded.

"So he holes up in the right spot and shoots Pike whichever side Pike's on," he said.

"He'll hole up on this side of the pass," I said.

"So he can get away into the hills," Virgil said.

"Otherwise, he got to run down onto the open land," I said.

"Agree?" Virgil said to Pony.

"Many places to hide uphill," Pony said. "Indian know the land. Ride light, just him and rifle. White men don't know land. Many equipment to carry."

"So that's where he'll run," Virgil said.

"If he run," Pony said.

"You think he won't?"

"I him, I won't," Pony said.

"Whadda you do?" Virgil said.

"Shoot many, then hide. They come after

me. I shoot some more and hide another place. Keep doing that. They run away, I go after them, shoot some more, until they get to flat land."

"You think they'll run?" I said.

"White man scared of Indians," Pony said. "Run away sometimes."

" 'Specially if the Indian gets Pike first," Virgil said.

"Indian want you, too, jefe," Pony said. "He stay till he get you."

"You think so?" Virgil said.

"He needs to kill you," Pony said. "You and Pike."

"Because?" Virgil said.

"You the ones," Pony said.

"How 'bout Everett?" Virgil said. "Or you?"

"You the ones," Pony said. "Pike and you."

"How do you know?" I said.

"Half Indian," Pony said. "Know how Indian people think."

Virgil nodded. He watched through his long glass as the posse plodded toward the hills. Then he collapsed the telescope and put it in his saddlebag.

"We may be all wrong," Virgil said.

"True," I said.

"But we might be right," Virgil said.

"True," I said.

"Let's mosey on down along this stream," he said. "See if we are."

48

We went as quietly as we could downhill along the stream. The stream gurgled softly, but maybe enough to mask our footsteps. Pony was out front a little; his moccasins made no sound at all. The rain added some sound, too. In front of us were two boulders, tilted against each other, glistening in the rain. Pony stopped behind them. We stopped. Pony pointed to his nose and sniffed at the air. We sniffed, too. Virgil began to nod. He put his mouth to my ear and said, "Horse shit." I smelled it, too. We moved up beside Pony.

"I'll go around the rocks left," Virgil said. "Pony goes around right. Everett, stay here with the eight-gauge."

I slid on my belly up onto the more slanted of the two boulders, took off my hat, and edged a look over the rim of the rock. Below there was a sort of hollow with some grass near the stream, then more rocks. The same smallish paint I'd seen before was tethered in the hollow, cropping the grass. There was no sign of the Indian. The horse wasn't big, but lying there a little above him I could see the thick muscles in his haunches and shoulders. He was strong. He'd go up this hill well. He had a conventional bridle on but no saddle.

Beyond the hollow were more rocks, and beyond them I could see the near rim of the pass. To my left, through the rain, I could see the posse coming closer. Below me the horse raised his head and looked at me. Probably smelled me. He stared at me, and I at him. He blew his breath out softly, then dropped his head and went back to eating the wet grass.

Then I saw the Indian.

He stepped out from the rocks with his rifle, looking around the hollow. He wore his black coat and hat. His face was painted black and I could see where the coat was open red stripes painted on his naked chest. I cocked the shotgun. He heard it and looked up at me, and Virgil stepped out from behind the rocks. He had his Colt but not his Winchester.

"Buffalo Calf," he said.

The Indian turned slowly and looked steadily at Virgil.

224

"You," he said.

"Me," Virgil said.

"You know my name," the Indian said.

"I do," Virgil said.

"What's your name," the Indian said.

"Virgil Cole."

"You are not with Pike," the Indian said.

"Nope."

"How many are you?"

"Everett up in the rocks," Virgil said. "Pony Flores over to your left."

The Indian nodded.

"Everett has a shotgun," the Indian said. "I heard both hammers cock."

"Eight-gauge," Virgil said.

The Indian nodded.

"I had planned to kill you," he said. "You and Pike."

Virgil nodded.

"Now, maybe, you will kill me," the Indian said.

"Maybe," Virgil said.

"I would wish to have killed Pike first," the Indian said.

"Why?" Virgil said.

"Things from our past," the Indian said.

"Put down the Winchester and we'll take you back to Brimstone," Virgil said.

"To a white-face jail," the Indian said.

"Yes."

"To be hanged by a white-face judge," the Indian said.

"Probably," Virgil said.

The Indian nodded.

"Virgil Cole," he said.

Virgil said nothing. The Indian bent over slowly and laid the rifle on the ground. Then he straightened and there was a big bowie knife in his hand. He came straight at Virgil. Virgil never moved, until, with no apparent hurry, he drew and fired and hit the Indian in the chest. The Indian kept coming. Virgil shot him twice more before he went down, the knife still in the Indian's hand. He crawled forward a little farther, then stopped. His whole body seemed to convulse with effort, and then it was still. He was dead at Virgil's feet. Virgil opened the cylinder, ejected the spent cartridges, and reloaded the Colt. Then he put the gun back in his holster and squatted on his heels and looked at Buffalo Calf.

49

We laid the Indian sideways over the back of his horse, and tied him in place. We got our own animals and went down the slope, leading the paint horse with Buffalo Calf's body. We rode for maybe half an hour on the flat plain before we came up to the posse. Pike was riding in the lead. When he saw us he stopped the posse and sat waiting for us, peering at us through the rain, until we got close enough for him to make everything out.

"You got to him first," Pike said to Virgil.

"We did," Virgil said.

Pike swung off his horse and walked to the dead Indian. He took hold of the Indian's hair and raised his head and looked at his face.

"Buffalo Calf," Pike said.

"Buffalo Calf," Virgil said.

Still holding the Indian's head up, Pike reached behind him and took a knife from his belt.

"No," Virgil said.

I never did understand how Virgil got that sound in his voice. But when he said "No," it was like the closing of an iron valve. Everything stopped.

"I want his scalp," Pike said.

"No," Virgil said.

Pike stepped back away from Virgil. I eased my eight-gauge out of its scabbard and rested it across my thigh. On Virgil's left, Pony looped his reins over the horn of his saddle. Pike looked at Virgil and then looked back at his posse.

"Virgil," he said. "There's twenty of us."

Virgil said, "Anybody puts a hand on a weapon, Pike, and I'll kill you."

"For a dead fucking red nigger," Pike said, "stole two women, killed three men, we know of?"

"Four," Virgil said.

"You'd fight all of us for that?"

"Be my plan," Virgil said.

Pike looked at me.

"Everett?" he said.

"I'm with Virgil," I said.

He looked to Virgil's left.

"You, Pony?" he said.

"Virgil," Pony said.

Pike backed off another step.

"You think you're good enough to kill me?" he said.

"Yes," Virgil said.

The rain was still coming down. Not hard but steady. The horses all had their heads down so it wouldn't get in their eyes and nostrils.

"You think you can kill us all?" Pike said.

"Be some of you left when we go down," Virgil said. "But you won't be one of 'em."

Virgil scanned the posse.

"Rest of you can try to figure which ones'll be left," he said.

We all sat our horses, except Pike, who still stood in front of Virgil. He took off his hat and held it at his side. The rain began to bead on his bald head. It might have been kind of a pleasant rain if I hadn't been wet since yesterday. Then, very deliberately, Pike put the knife back in his belt. He shook the water off his hat and put it back on. He grinned.

"Just a damn Comanche buck," Pike said. "No need for white men to die over him."

Virgil didn't speak.

"Hell, Virgil," Pike said. "We'll all ride back together."

"We'll trail along behind you," Virgil said.

"You don't trust me, Virgil?"

"Never did," Virgil said. "You're too

damned jolly for me."

Pike laughed.

"I don't think you can beat me anyway," he said.

"Never know till we've tried it," Virgil said.

Pike laughed again and swung his bulk up onto his horse.

I put the eight-gauge back in its scabbard. Pike turned the posse. We fell in behind it.

And we headed back to Brimstone.

50

It was hard to say if the Ostermueller girls, mother and daughter, had a reaction to Buffalo Calf's death. Mary Beth was drunk now, nearly all the time. And Laurel still didn't speak, except, now and then, in a whisper, to Virgil. Virgil didn't report what she said.

Laurel did, however, take to hanging around the sheriff's office, first only when Virgil was there, but after a time, when either of us was there. She'd come in and sweep up, and make fresh coffee, and sit quietly on the old couch and look out the window. She never spoke. But when Virgil was there, she watched him nearly all the time.

Mary Beth, when she was sober enough, was making a living on her back in Pike's Palace. It wasn't much of a living because she wasn't taking very good care of herself, so she was the whore of last resort most of the time. She was often too drunk to per-form. What little money she did make went for booze.

Virgil and I were sitting on the front porch in the bright morning, drinking some of Laurel's fresh coffee, while she swept up inside. The sun was warm after days of rain, and the town was full of energy.

"What'd you do with the Indian's horse?" I said.

"Gave him to Pony," Virgil said.

"What'd Pony do with him?" I said. "Damn thing was barely broke."

"Pony shot him," Virgil said. "So Buffalo Calf would have something to ride in the spirit world."

"Pony believe that?"

"Don't know," Virgil said.

"But Buffalo Calf probably did," I said.

"I guess," Virgil said.

"Pony ain't so far from the wickiup him-self," I said.

" 'Pears not," Virgil said.

We were quiet while we watched a team of red-and-white Ayrshire oxen pull a big freight wagon up Arrow Street.

"Nice-looking team," I said.

"Me and Allie been talking 'bout Laurel," Virgil said.

I nodded.

"She ain't getting no mothering that's worth anything," Virgil said. " 'Cept what she gets from Allie."

I nodded.

"We want to take her in with us," he said.

"And put her in my room," I said.

"Figure you can bunk in one of the cells," Virgil said.

"Fine with me," I said. "You talk to Laurel about it yet?"

"No. Thought I better clear it with you first."

"Girl that age shouldn't be on her own," I said. " 'Specially after the things happened to her."

"Allie can sort of look after her," Virgil said. "Might be good for Allie, too."

"Kid makes good coffee," I said. "Maybe she can cook."

"Be like finding gold, if she can," Virgil said.

"Percival been bothering her?" I said.

Virgil didn't say anything.

"You promised her you wouldn't tell nobody what she told you," I said.

"Yep."

"You promise anything else?"

"Yep."

"You promised her you wouldn't do nothing," I said.

Virgil shrugged.

"So, if Percival's been poking her, and she told you about it, you can't say nothing about it, and you can't shoot him."

Virgil shrugged.

"I didn't make no promise," I said.

"You give your word," Virgil said, "you don't weasel on it."

"You mean you can't let me do nothing."

"I don't want no one bothering Brother Percival," Virgil said.

"Okay."

"Time comes to bother him," Virgil said, "I'll do it."

"You can bother hell out of someone, you really set your mind to it," I said.

"I know," Virgil said, and went into the office to talk with Laurel.

51

We developed a routine. Every morning Allie would drop Laurel off at the office, leave me some biscuits for breakfast, and then hustle away on God's business. Or Brother Percival's. Or one and the same. The biscuits would have stopped a bullet. Laurel would make coffee, sweep up the office, and sit on the couch. I would soak the biscuits in the coffee until they had softened up enough to eat. When the weather was good, I took my breakfast outside. Virgil usually saddled up and did a sweep of the town to start the day, so for a while it was just me and Laurel.

The third week we did this, Laurel brought some corn cakes for breakfast. They were still warm. It was worth sleeping in the jail.

"Allie make this?" I said.

She shook her head.

"Virgil?"

She shook her head. She didn't smile, but

I thought for a moment she might. I picked up the corn cakes and a cup of coffee and went out onto the porch. It was early, and the streets were still empty. I sat down. A coyote came out of the alley between the sheriff's office and the bank next door. He paused in the middle of Arrow Street and looked at me. I looked back. Then he turned and trotted on across the street and into the alley across the street. Always good forage in a growing town. I sipped some coffee. There was a lot of sugar in it. Behind me the office door opened and Laurel came out and sat in the chair beside me.

"Want a corn cake?" I said.

She nodded. I held the plate toward her. She broke off a piece of one cake and held it in her hand. I took a piece and set the plate on the floor of the porch beside my chair. She took a very small bite. I ate some of mine.

"You cook better than Allie," I said.

She chewed her corn cake.

" 'Course, so do I," I said.

She took another small bite. She sat straight in the chair with her feet flat on the floor and her knees together.

"Your mother teach you to cook?" I said.

I wasn't looking at her, so I didn't know if she nodded. I proceeded as if she had.

"Did a good job," I said. "Taught you how to sit like a lady, too."

I glanced at her. She was looking straight ahead.

"Hard now," I said. "That she's having so much trouble. Hard for you. Hard for her."

Laurel was silent. Up the street a wagon pulled up outside of Pike's Palace. The driver jumped down and tied up at the rail outside. There was a piano and a piano bench on the back of the wagon. In a minute Brother Percival came around the corner with Allie. Behind them came Choctaw Brown. Percival helped Allie into the wagon and she began to play loudly, some sort of unrecognizable church music. He climbed in beside her and rested his elbow on the piano. A few early drunks wandered out of the Palace and stared at the wagon. Virgil rode around the corner of Sixth Street and came down behind them and stopped and sat his horse to listen.

"Pike's Palace," Percival bellowed. "A palace of debauchery, a stench of whores and poisonous whiskey, a stench of sin, like rotting flesh, odious to God and to all who love Him."

Allie played some more. Choctaw leaned against the wall next to the door of Pike's Palace and looked faintly amused. Pike made no appearance. After a while, Percival stopped shouting. Allie stopped playing. They climbed down from the wagon and headed up Fifth Street with Choctaw trailing behind them. The wagon driver untied from the rail and climbed up on his wagon and drove back down Fifth Street. Virgil turned his horse and walked him down the street toward us.

I looked at Laurel.

"Allie don't play the piano so good, either," I said.

Laurel nodded almost vigorously.

When Virgil arrived and dismounted, Laurel jumped up and went in and got him some coffee.

"Thank you," Virgil said. "You sit in the chair, Laurel."

She shook her head. Virgil nodded as if to himself.

"There's a chair beside my desk," he said to Laurel. "Would you go get it and bring it out here?"

She nodded.

When she came out with it, Virgil said, "Put it there, between my chair and Everett."

She did.

Virgil sat in the chair she'd vacated for him. He looked at Laurel and pointed at

238

the chair she'd just brought out.

"Now sit in it," he said to her.

She stared at him. Then she sat down between us.

52

"Big doings up at the Palace," Virgil said.

I nodded.

"Surprising," I said.

"Uh-huh," Virgil said. "Kinda thought there was something going on between Percival and Pike."

"Looks like there is, but it ain't what we thought," I said.

"Or it was what we thought, and now it ain't," Virgil said.

"Choctaw's still trailing along," I said.

"Yep."

I watched a cluster of sparrows fluttering around the dried horse manure in the street. Virgil drank his coffee. A fancy little carriage went down the street past us, pulled by a sorrel horse with a black mane and tail. The sparrows flew up as it went by and settled directly back to breakfast when it was gone.

Laurel leaned over and pulled at Virgil's

sleeve. He put his head down, and she whispered to him. He nodded. She whispered some more. He nodded again and whispered to her. She looked at me for a moment. Then she nodded.

"Laurel says Pike and Percival had a big argument. I asked her if I could tell you about it, and she said yes."

"Thank you, Laurel," I said.

"Percival and Pike got together pretty often, Laurel says. Pike would come over to the compound, and he and Percival would have a drink together in Percival's office, and they'd talk awhile. . . ."

Virgil looked at Laurel.

"Can I tell the next part?" he said.

Laurel looked at me silently for a moment, then nodded her head.

"Then Pike would visit with Mary Beth."

Laurel was watching me. There wasn't anything to say. I nodded and looked at her and smiled. She kept looking at me.

"Just before Laurel moved in with Allie and me," Virgil said, "Pike came over, they went to the office, and after a while there was a lot of yelling and the door yanked open and Pike came out. He said a bad word to Percival, and Percival says, 'My kingdom is not of this earth.' "

He looked at Laurel again.

"That right, Laurel?"

She nodded.

" 'My kingdom is not of this earth,' " Virgil said.

I shrugged.

"Taking this God thing pretty serious," I said.

"Probably more than Pike does," Virgil said.

"Probably," I said.

"And Pike speaks another bad word," Virgil said. "And walks off without visiting Mary Beth."

"And now Percival is outside his place preaching against him," I said.

"Worked on the other saloons," Virgil said.

"I kinda thought that was the deal," I said. "Percival closes down all the other saloons. Pike gets all the business."

"I kinda thought that, too," Virgil said.

"And Choctaw?" I said.

"Kinda thought he was Pike's man," Virgil said. "Keeping an eye on Percival."

"Or keeping somebody from killing him while he put them out of business for Pike," I said.

"Job might be changing," Virgil said.

"Might."

"Guess we'll see," Virgil said.

"We got a side in this?" I said.

"Depends on what this is," Virgil said.

"Say this is some sort of battle between Pike and Percival," I said.

"Well," Virgil said. "We the law."

"Yeah, and one law knows a lot more about this than the other law," I said. "Why I'm asking."

"Let's await developments," Virgil said.

He stood.

"Can't sit here all day," he said.

He took his coffee cup and walked into the office. Laurel stood up at once and walked in behind him. I looked after them and smiled.

I was good enough only when Virgil wasn't around . . . sorta like with Allie.

53

The piano mounted on the wagon expanded Allie's horizon. She'd taken to driving it herself and parking at every hitching post in town. She'd climb back, sit on the piano bench, and play hymns and sing by herself, without Percival. Today she was doing it right across from the sheriff's office.

"That's a painful noise," Virgil said.

"Can't you do something 'bout it?" I said to Virgil.

"Keeps her from cooking," Virgil said.

We were sitting on the porch, Virgil, Laurel, and me.

"Yes," I said. "I s'pose it does."

I looked at Laurel and put my fingers in my ears. She dropped her head, and in a moment, put her fingers in her ears, and looked cautiously up to see if I was looking. I smiled at her. She didn't smile back, but she didn't look away.

People stopped as they passed her and

listened. I suspected it was in disbelief. Between hymns she climbed down with a collection plate and passed it among them. If they gave her anything she would say, "God bless you." Then she climbed back up on the wagon and played some more and sang some more. I couldn't tell if it was the same hymns or new ones. They were loud but unvaried. After a while, when no more people came to the wagon, she loosed the team from its hitching post, got back in the wagon seat, waved at us across the street, and drove to a new location.

"You think she believes all this stuff?" I said to Virgil.

"I never quite understood Allie," Virgil said.

"And now you do?" I said.

"I been thinking 'bout it ever since we took her out of Placido," Virgil said.

Laurel was sitting very still and very erect, watching Virgil's face as he talked.

"Always loved her, even when she cheated on me, which, certain sure, she's done a lot of," Virgil said. "Still love her. Don't know why. What I read, I guess that's how it is. You love somebody, you love 'em."

Laurel was staring at him.

" 'Course, I was mad at her a lot," he said. "You know anything 'bout that, Everett?"

"Never been in love," I said. "Liked a lot of women. Never loved one."

"That's too bad," Virgil said. "When it's right, it feels real good."

"Feel right often?" I said.

"Not too often with Allie," Virgil said. "But . . ."

Laurel had probably never heard a man talk about such things in her whole life. Virgil didn't talk about feelings much, because I'm not so sure he had many. But when he cared to, he would talk about anything he felt like talking about. Laurel seemed immobilized, listening to him.

"One of the things I come to see," Virgil said, "is that Allie believes whatever she needs to believe. And when she don't need to, she believes something else."

I nodded.

"She needs a man taking care of her," I said.

"Yep."

"You ain't it," I said.

"I'm taking care of her," Virgil said. "Just not . . ."

He looked at Laurel.

"You know," he said.

"Which means she can't trust you to take care of her."

"Sure she can."

"But she don't know it, 'less you and she are, ah, taking care of business, she don't feel like she got any control."

"Maybe so," Virgil said.

"Ain't you, it may as well be God, I guess."

"Yep."

Laurel leaned close to Virgil and whispered to him. He listened and nodded. Then he looked at me.

"Laurel told me she understands what we're talking about, and she don't mind if we say fuck when we need to." Virgil's face showed nothing as he spoke.

I nodded.

"Thank you, Laurel," I said.

54

It was late afternoon. I came back from my turn walking the town and found Allie in the office with Virgil. Laurel sat on the couch silently. Virgil sat at his desk. Allie was on the couch next to Laurel, leaning forward, her hands clasped tightly in her lap.

"Want me to come back?" I said.

Virgil shook his head and pointed at a chair. I sat.

"I wanted to tell her here, with you," Allie said to Virgil.

Virgil nodded.

"I just found out," Allie said.

Virgil nodded.

"Laurel's mother killed herself last night," Allie said.

She put her hand on Laurel's knee. Laurel didn't move. She was looking hard at Virgil. Virgil stood and walked to the couch. He gestured for Allie to sit at his desk, and when she stood he took her place beside Laurel. Laurel edged slightly toward him and let her shoulder touch his.

"I'm sorry," Virgil said to her.

She nodded.

"But your life ain't gonna change much," Virgil said. "You been with us, and you'll be with us. We'll take care of you."

She nodded. Her face had not changed. She remained motionless. Then she leaned toward Virgil and whispered to him. He listened. Then he nodded.

"Probably is," he said.

"I got something else I got to do, Virgil," Allie said.

Virgil nodded.

"I got to tell you things," Allie said.

Virgil nodded again.

"If we going to take care of this child, I got to start clean for her," Allie said.

Virgil waited.

"Brother Percival is in cahoots with Pike," Allie said.

Virgil nodded.

"Pike agreed to let him have his crusade if he closed down the other saloons and not Pike's," Allie said.

Virgil nodded.

"Then Pike gets all the saloon profit in town," Allie said. "And Brother Percival's church gets to be bigger and bigger."

"Kinda figured a lot of that," Virgil said.

"But it's changed," Allie said. "Percival is going to close down Pike."

All of us were silent for a time.

Then Virgil said, "How do you know?"

"That's the shameful part, Virgil," Allie said. "I been with him. Even after he bothered this child, I been with him."

"I kinda knew that, too, Allie," Virgil said.

"How'd you know that?" Allie said.

Virgil didn't answer.

"Percival would be with me and he would drink and he would tell me things," Allie said. "He's crazy, Virgil. I think he actually thinks he's God."

"Probably ain't," Virgil said.

Allie went on, in a kind of rush.

"He says he gets Pike outta the way . . . and you and Everett . . . says he will turn the town into a new Bethlehem."

"He think Pike's going to go along with this?" Virgil said.

"No," Allie said. "He knows there'll be a fight. He sent Choctaw Brown out to hire more deacons."

"He thinks Choctaw's with him on this?"

"Yes."

"Choctaw's with Pike," Virgil said.

"How do you know?" Allie said.

Virgil shook his head and didn't answer.

"I had to tell you," Allie said. "I knew I'd have to say I was with Percival, but you had to know. He said he was going to get rid of you, too. I couldn't let that happen."

"No," Virgil said.

He looked at Laurel.

"I am hard to get rid of," he said. "You shouldn't worry about it."

She whispered in his ear.

"Me 'n Everett," Virgil said. "Like always."

She whispered to him again. He listened and nodded slowly.

"Good idea," he said. "Everett, see if you can find Pony Flores, if you would."

Which I did.

55

"Got reason to think there'll be trouble between Percival and Pike," Virgil said to Pony.

"Sí," Pony said.

"I think Pike will chew Percival up and spit him out," Virgil said.

"Sí," Pony said.

"But before he does," Virgil said, "Everett and me may be in the middle of it."

Pony nodded.

"Where do you stand?" Virgil said.

Pony pointed at Virgil.

"Okay," Virgil said. "Ball goes up, somebody gotta be looking out for Laurel."

Pony nodded and pointed at his chest.

"You all right with Pony?" Virgil said to Laurel.

She nodded slowly.

"Might keep an eye on Allie, too," Virgil said.

"Like mother chicken," Pony said.

"How come you're not sticking with Pike?" I said.

Pony nodded at Laurel.

"Chiquita," he said.

I nodded.

"You know anything 'bout all this?" Virgil said.

"Pike know 'bout Percival," Pony said.

"Choctaw?" I said.

"Everybody know Choctaw work for Pike," Pony said.

" 'Cept Percival," Virgil said.

"Percival crazy," Pony said.

"Pike knows that, too?" Virgil said.

"Everybody know that, too."

" 'Cept Percival," Virgil said.

"Pike say he don't mind if you boys get killed, either," Pony said.

"Be his town then," I said. "You think Pike got the outfit to do the job?"

"Percival? Sure," Pony said. "You boys and me?" He grinned and shook his head.

" 'Less he's hiring some new boys," I said. "Choctaw's the best he's got."

"Choctaw's good," Virgil said.

"Good as you?" I said.

Virgil said, "Subject to proof."

"Pike the best," Pony said.

"Might be," Virgil said.

"Is," Pony said. "Seen him."

"Maybe we'll find out," Virgil said.

"Pike said he was gonna kill you," Allie said.

Her voice seemed hoarse and small, as if she were forcing it out through a narrow opening.

We all looked at her.

"Who'd he say that to?" Virgil asked her.

"Me," she said. "Men tend to brag when . . . you know."

Virgil stared at her as if he were startled. Which wasn't possible, because Virgil Cole was never startled.

"Allie," he said. " 'Stead of telling me who you been with, be easier if you gave me a short list of men you haven't."

"Wasn't with him often," Allie said. "Percival used to give me to him once in a while when he'd come over, and they'd be drinking."

Virgil stood and walked to the office door and looked out at the street for a while. Laurel watched him closely.

Without taking his eyes off the street, Virgil said, "We got to go over this, Allie, all of it, you, me, Laurel. But now ain't the time."

He turned slowly from the door and looked at Allie.

"Right now you got one thing to do. You look out for Laurel. You and Pony. You do what Pony says and you don't ask questions and you don't think. You do what he says."

"I am trying to help, Virgil, honest to God. I'm a different woman. I only want to help."

"You hear what I told you," Virgil said.

"Yes."

Virgil walked back and sat beside Laurel again.

"You too, Laurel," he said. "When it all starts, you do what Pony says, just like it was me."

She nodded.

"Can you talk with him?" Virgil said.

She shook her head.

"Okay," Virgil said. "Pony ain't much of a talker, anyway."

56

Virgil was a bear on exercising the horses. Most days we'd ride at least one town patrol on them, and every couple of days we'd take them out and breeze them along the river. This day, as we rode back toward town, Virgil reined in for a moment and sat looking across the river where we'd first seen the Indian.

"Wonder what it was," Virgil said. " 'Tween that Indian and Pike."

"Something that mattered," I said. "He wanted to do more than just kill him."

Virgil nodded.

"Thinking about it," Virgil said, "I figure them arrows was all for Pike."

"Yep."

"Means Pike knew who it was all the time," Virgil said. "Since they found that steer."

"Yep."

"Mighta helped if he told us," Virgil said.

256

"Would," I said.

We moved the horses forward, letting them walk now, taking our time.

"Think it'll go like Allie told us?" I said.

"You know Pike," Virgil said. "You know Percival. Whadda you think?"

"It'll go like Allie told us."

Virgil nodded.

"Be nice if they wiped each other out," I said.

"Be nice," Virgil said.

"How we going to play it?" I said.

"Stay out of the way," Virgil said. "Contain it. When one side wins, we deal with them."

"What you gonna do about Allie?" I said.

"Don't know about Allie," Virgil said.

"Hell," I said. "Allie don't know about Allie."

"Probably not," Virgil said. "But I know we can't raise no fifteen-year-old girl without a woman."

"Don't have to be Allie," I said.

"Got no better choice at the moment," Virgil said.

"No," I said. "We don't."

The horses took us slowly back into town, and on down Arrow Street toward the livery stable. The town seemed like it always did. Busy. Lotta people on the street. Kinda prosperous. The Church of the Brotherhood

257

was closed and silent. No organ music. Allie wasn't playing there anymore. At Pike's Palace, several of his associates were lingering outside on the porch, wearing sidearms.

We left the horses at the stable and walked to the office. We dipped some water from the barrel, and drank, and sat on the front porch and looked at things.

"So we sit and await developments?" I said.

"Nope," Virgil said. "I think we go right at 'em."

"Good," I said. "I hate awaiting developments."

57

There was a new lookout at Pike's Palace, a tall, thin guy with striped pants and a shotgun on his lap. I went and stood against the wall near him with the eight-gauge while Virgil went to talk with Pike at the bar. The lookout wasn't happy about me standing there. He looked at Pike. Pike shrugged faintly, and the lookout settled back.

"Why the heavy ordnance, Virgil," Pike said.

"Oh, Everett's forgetful," Virgil said. "Afraid if he lays that thing down, he'll forget where he put it."

"Beer?" Pike said.

"Sure thing," Virgil said.

Pike looked at me. I shook my head. The bartender set a beer in front of Virgil, and one for Pike.

"This a social call?" Pike said.

Virgil sipped his beer and put it down.

"Chance for a free beer, mostly," Virgil said.

"Anytime, Virgil," Pike said.

He was wearing a dark suit and a red tie, and carried a Colt.

"Who's the new lookout," Virgil said.

"Abner Noonan," Pike said. "Was with me in the Army."

"Hearda him," Virgil said. "Was in Laredo for a while."

"Good memory," Pike said. "Yep, that's Abner."

"Replacing Kirby and J.D.," Virgil said.

"Yes," Pike said.

Virgil looked absently around the room.

"Got some other new faces," Virgil said.

Pike grinned.

"Just keeping the staff up to level," he said.

"Too bad 'bout Kirby and J.D.," Virgil said.

"Was," Pike said.

"You know, Pike," Virgil said. "I was thinking 'bout that Indian killed them."

I smiled to myself. Virgil could be as direct as anyone alive, or he could, for his own reasons, go around the Gulf of Mexico and come in the back way when he felt like it. This was going to be the back way.

"What were you thinking?" Pike said.

"What was that boy's name," Virgil said.

"Buffalo Calf."

"They all got names," Pike said.

"Well, you know, it don't matter," Virgil said. "But there musta been something between you two."

"Me and the Indian?" Pike said. "Why do you care?"

"Just a curious fella," Virgil said. "Hate to know half a thing. I know it don't matter, and it ain't official or anything, and Buffalo Calf been disposed of. But . . . I keep thinking on it."

Pike grinned.

"Like an itch you can't scratch," Pike said.

"That's what it's like," Virgil said.

He sipped some more beer.

"Oh, hell, Virgil," Pike said. "I was a lieutenant trying to make captain. Everett over there probably knows what that's like."

"I do," I said. "One reason I quit."

"I had a patrol out, me, a sergeant, and twelve troopers. Caught some Apaches out in the open. They were moving camp, had stuff on travois, mostly women and children, a few bucks, and we cleaned them out. We were still using the breech loaders, and it was slow, so I told the troopers to use their sabers. It was a bloody mess, but it went faster and we killed them all."

Pike drank some beer.

"So I'm surveying the mess." Pike grinned. "And thinking about my second bar, and something hits me on the shoulder and falls to the ground. I look and it's a toy arrow, and another one hits me, and I see this little Indian kid, maybe nine, ten, covered with blood, kneeling behind some dead squaw, shooting at me with his toy bow and arrow. One of the troopers goes and grabs him and is gonna cut his throat, and the little bastard was so mean and so brave, I say, 'Don't kill him.' Sergeant looks at me like I'm crazy, but we drag him along with us back to Tucson, and I put him into the Indian school there. All the ride back to Tucson, he looks at me, and when I checked on him every once in a while at the school, he don't say nothing, just looks at me. Does good at the school. Speaks English good, read, write, all that shit. And the day he's eighteen he's gone and no one sees him again. Then ten years later, that steer shows up dead with the toy arrow."

"That why you gave us Pony to track?"

"Felt bad 'bout them women," Pike said. "Sorta felt a little responsible, I suppose."

"Sure," Virgil said.

"Last break I ever gave anybody," Pike said. "And that was one too many."

"Thank you, Pike," Virgil said. "I'll sleep better."

"Sure thing," Pike said.

"You expecting trouble with Percival?" Virgil said.

"Nothing we can't handle," Pike said.

"But you're expecting some."

"Percival's crazy," Pike said. "I won't let him close me down."

"Hey, Everett," Virgil said. "What's that thing where you attack first to stop somebody from attacking you."

"Preemptive strike," I said.

"You ain't thinking 'bout any preemptive strikes," Virgil said.

"He tries to close me down," Pike said. "And I'll do what's needed."

"Probably can't prevent the trouble," Virgil said. "But I'd like to contain it."

"How you gonna contain it?" Pike said.

"Just don't do more than is needed," Virgil said.

"Who's going to decide that?" Pike said.

"That would be me," Virgil said. "And Everett."

58

"Worked a town in Oklahoma once," Virgil said as we walked along Arrow Street toward The Church of the Brotherhood. "Had one of them Indian schools. Everybody working their ass off to teach these kids to be what they weren't."

"Buffalo Calf wasn't a quitter," I said. "Musta taken him ten years to find Pike."

"Yep."

"Then he wanted to stretch it out," I said. "So it wouldn't be over too quick."

"All he had," Virgil said.

He paused and looked at a dress hanging in the window of a shop.

"You a pretty smart fella, Everett."

"Sure," I said.

"Went to the Academy and all."

"Yep."

"Think she'll ever change?" he said.

I knew he meant Allie.

"Folks generally don't," I said.

264

"No," Virgil said.

He kept looking at the dress.

"You?" I said.

"Change?" he said. " 'Bout Allie?"

"Yep."

"Maybe," he said. "This time I think I could haze her off."

"But," I said.

"Got that girl to take care of."

"There's other women in the world," I said.

"Not right at the moment," Virgil said.

"You love Allie?" I said.

"I might."

"And maybe Laurel's a good excuse," I said.

"Maybe," Virgil said.

He turned from the window and looked at me.

"And maybe I'm glad I got an excuse," he said. "Either way, we gonna keep her for now."

"Take care of Laurel," I said.

"Yes."

I nodded.

"Wasn't planning on no daughter," I said.

"Nope."

We walked on toward the church. It was a warm day, with some wind that kicked up the dust in the street in little swirls and bothered the parasols that some of the ladies carried.

"Laurel might change her," Virgil said.

"Maybe," I said.

"I think she will," Virgil said.

I didn't say anything.

"I'll only say this to you, Everett," Virgil said. " 'Cause I don't mind so much looking like a fool to you. But I believe her this time."

"And them other men?" I said.

"Got nothing to do with me," Virgil said.

I nodded. We walked on. We could see The Church of the Brotherhood ahead of us. There were several deacons standing around outside wearing Colts.

" 'Less it keeps happening," Virgil said. "Can't take that no more."

"Good," I said.

Virgil nodded and stopped outside the church.

"Howdy, boys," he said. "We come to see Brother Percival."

59

We sat with Percival in a pew near the back of the church.

"I've not seen Allie lately," Percival said. "Is she well?"

"She's busy with Laurel Ostermueller," Virgil said.

"Ah, yes, how tragic, the abduction, then her mother killing herself."

"You fucking them," Virgil said.

"If you came to be abusive," Percival said, "then this conversation is over."

"Believe you fucked Allie some, too."

Percival rose to his feet.

"You're appalling," he said to Virgil.

"I am, for a fact," Virgil said. "You got any plans to close Pike down?"

It was moving a little fast for Brother Percival. He shook his head slightly as if to clear it.

"Pike?" he said.

"Yeah. You planning on running him out

like you done all the other saloon owners?" Virgil said.

" 'Saloon owners,' " Percival said. "You say it as if it were ordinary. Every one of the sins that accumulated in those hellholes that I closed has re-formed and erupted in Pike's Palace. It is the ultimate cesspool of corruption, and it is poisoning the town."

"That sound like yes to you, Everett?" Virgil said.

"Seems so to me," I said.

"You think Pike gonna let you close him down?" Virgil said.

"An armed and muscular Christianity cannot be defeated," Percival answered.

He always sounded to me like he was recycling his own sermons, which he probably was.

"I wouldn't count too much on Choctaw," Virgil said.

"I rely on my Father in heaven," Percival said.

"Probably better than Choctaw," Virgil said.

Percival looked down at us with contempt, dirtied as we were with mortality.

"Is there a purpose to this visit?" Percival said.

"Ain't planning to prevent you doing what you going to do," Virgil said. "Nor Pike from

268

answering you back. You both got the right. But these things have a way of spillin' over, and I don't want that to happen."

"What you want, Deputy," Percival said, "what either of you wants, doesn't matter, I am not governed by you and your laws. My allegiance is to a far greater power, and what He and I will do is not open to debate."

"Well, Brother P.," Virgil said. "What me and Everett want matters to us, and when it matters enough, we are pretty good at making it matter to other people. I want you to keep this thing between you and Pike between you and Pike."

Percival stared down at Virgil without speaking.

"And," Virgil said, "if things get outta hand, I'm gonna shoot you. Everett might shoot you, too."

Percival continued to stare down at us. Then without a word he turned and stormed away down the center aisle of the church. Virgil and I watched him go.

"Think we scared him?" I said.

" 'Fraid not," Virgil said.

"Him or the Heavenly Father," I said.

"Neither," Virgil said.

60

It was like a summer storm approaching. The atmosphere tightened; I could feel the tension crackling. There was no thunder yet, or lightning, but I could feel it lurking. I knew it was coming. So did everyone else. There were more men with guns standing around. There were fewer people on the streets. The people who were on the streets walked faster. The dogs seemed to slink a little. The horses seemed edgy. Everyone seemed somehow wound a little tighter. Except Virgil. As always, he remained entirely Virgil Cole, regardless of what was going on around him.

"Gonna be one hell a deluge," I said, as we walked in the evening back to Allie's house.

"Deluge?" Virgil said. "Like rain?"

"Just thinking out loud," I said.

Virgil shook his head.

"You're kinda strange sometimes, Everett," Virgil said.

"Yeah," I said. "I know."

Pony was sitting in a rocker on Allie's front porch with a Winchester in his lap. Laurel sat on a straight chair next to him.

"Where's Allie?" Virgil said.

"Cook supper," Pony said.

"Uh-oh," Virgil said.

Pony shrugged.

"We'll be here for a while," I said to Pony, "you want to go up to Pike's or whatever."

"Good," Pony said. "Maybe eat."

I grinned.

"Better hurry," I said. "I think she's coming."

Pony stood and leaned the Winchester against the doorjamb.

"Watch the rifle for me," he said.

Virgil nodded.

"Don't go too far," Virgil said.

Pony nodded and walked off toward Arrow Street. Virgil sat next to Laurel.

"You know something?" I said to Virgil.

"Just a feeling," Virgil said. "Air's kinda tight."

I didn't say anything. Allie came out in an apron. It wasn't much of an apron, as far as keeping gravy off your dress. But it was cute-looking, and she looked cute in it.

"Supper's ready," she said.

271

She was making progress. The food wasn't good. But nothing was burned, and we ate as much of it as we could so as not to hurt her feelings. We were back on the porch letting it digest when Pony came silently out of the darkness. Virgil had heard him, I could tell, because he had shifted forward slightly in his chair to clear his gun hand.

"Percival," he said. "At Pike's. All lined up. Singing church music."

"Sounds like it's gonna start," I said.

Virgil nodded. He looked at Pony and jerked his head at the women. Pony nodded and picked up his Winchester and sat down beside Laurel. Virgil stood and went into the house. In a moment he came out with another Colt. One with a shorter barrel. A banker's gun. He gave it to Allie.

"Showed you how to shoot," Virgil said. "You need to, shoot."

Allie didn't say anything. But she nodded and took the gun. Virgil picked up his Winchester. I picked up the eight-gauge.

Virgil looked at the women.

"Be back soon," he said.

They both nodded. And we started up toward Arrow Street.

61

There was low cloud cover preventing the moon and stars from being visible. On Arrow Street there were some coal-oil lamps. But the clouds made the side streets very black. I could barely see Virgil beside me. We could hear singing ahead, and when we reached Arrow Street, we could see the singers, Percival and his people, lined up opposite Pike's Palace, holding torches, singing "The Battle Hymn of the Republic."

Mine eyes have seen the glory . . .

"Jesus," Virgil said.

. . . of the coming of the Lord . . .

At the center of the line and a little forward was Brother Percival, with Choctaw Brown beside him. Brother Percival was singing at full throat. Choctaw was silent.

. . . trampling out the vintage . . .

On the front porch of Pike's Palace stood maybe a dozen men, all armed. Pike was there, and Abner Noonan, the new shotgun lookout, was beside Pike. I recognized most of the rest from seeing them in the Palace. There were people I didn't see. I knew Pike had at least twenty.

. . . where the grapes of wrath are stored . . .

"Where's the rest of Pike's people," I said.

Virgil nodded at the photographer's shop across the way. There was an alley on each side of the shop, leading to Market Street. In both alley mouths I could see men.

"If the ball goes up," I said, "Pike'll cut them to pieces."

"Yep."

"We gonna do anything 'bout that?" I said.

"Nope."

"Why not."

"What we gain ain't commensurate with what we might lose," Virgil said.

He'd waited all this time to use his new word.

"So we lie back here in the weeds and watch," I said.

"We do," Virgil said.

"And if they start shooting, when it's over, we'll have that many fewer people to deal with."

"Exactly right," Virgil said.

. . . loosed the fateful lightning of His terrible swift sword . . .

Percival's people plodded on through the

"Battle Hymn," with the torches dancing in the night air, and Pike and his men motionless and silent on the porch before them.

. . . glory, glory, hallelujah . . .

When they finished, everything was quiet. I could hear the torches burning. Then Percival stepped forward and up onto the porch. He stood directly in front of Pike.

"I am here to do my Father's will," he said. "I am here to close this pestilence and drive you from this town."

"I'm not going to fuck with this, Percival," Pike said. "You people bother me and a lot of you will get hurt."

"You think we fear you?" Percival said.

"I think you should," Pike said.

"Because we are godly does not mean we are weak," Percival said.

He raised his fists in some sort of boxing stance. Pike looked at him in mock amazement.

"What the fuck are you doing?" he said.

Percival punched him on the chin. It took Pike by surprise and made him rock back on his heels for a moment. Then he exploded. He lunged his mass into Percival's, and half turned and clubbed Percival across the side of the head. It turned Percival and sent him staggering backward and off the porch, where he landed facedown in the

275

dirt. A low sound came from the assembled torchbearers. Percival rolled around in the dirt for a moment in some sort of frenzy, then turned and, sitting in the street, faced Pike. He was covered with dirt. He leveled his arm at Pike, pointing with his forefinger.

"Choctaw," he screamed. "Kill him."

Choctaw looked down at Percival for a minute with a half-smile and shook his head. Then he stepped up onto the porch and stood beside Pike and Abner. Percival was on his hands and knees in the street now, staring up at the men on the porch.

"Judas," he said.

Then he scrambled around and screamed at his deacons.

"Kill them. Kill all of them."

The deacons didn't have a chance. Abner killed two. Choctaw killed two. Pike killed three, and a half-dozen others went down, caught in the crossfire from both sides of the street, before the rest broke and ran. When it was over, Percival was still crouched in the street. The abandoned torches flickered and guttered out. The darkness closed in a little.

Pike looked down at him without speaking. Percival didn't move. He stayed on his hands and knees, his head hanging. Pike climbed down from the porch and walked over to him and kicked him. Percival fell on his side and doubled over.

"You be outta this town before the sun comes up tomorrow," Pike said. "Or I'll kill you."

Pike turned and walked back up onto the porch and across it and into his saloon. Percival remained curled up in the street.

On the porch Choctaw said in a voice meant to sound like Percival, "Choctaw, kill him." Then he laughed and followed Pike inside.

Percival stayed lying in the street for a while, with his knees drawn up. Then he got to his hands and knees for a time, his head hanging. Then slowly he got to his feet, and stood and looked around. The street was empty except for me and Virgil and the dead bodies of Percival's supporters. It must have looked even emptier to Percival. If he saw us, he didn't care. After a time he turned and began to trudge like a man exhausted down Arrow Street toward his church. Nothing else moved in the silent darkness.

"That it for the night?" I said to Virgil.

"Let's watch a little longer," Virgil said.

"For what?" I said.

Virgil shrugged.

"Percival's crazy," Virgil said.

"And we want to see how crazy," I said.

"Don't hurt to see," Virgil said.

I nodded. We stood. Percival went into the church and closed the doors behind him. A coyote trotted out from one of the alleys and sniffed the corpses. Virgil shooed him away. The coyote slunk back into the alley, looking resentful. Time passes slowly when you are doing nothing in the dark. We stood for a long time, I think. But finally, there was a kind of explosion from the church, and flames burst out of the front door. By the time we got there the building was fully burning. We had to stop maybe twenty feet away, as the heat made a barrier we couldn't penetrate. We heard a single gunshot from somewhere in the fire, and then nothing, except the sound of the fire as it consumed The Church of the Brotherhood and, probably, the dead body of its pastor.

62

The day after was bright and still. The volunteer fire brigade hadn't been able to save the church, which Percival appeared to have soaked with coal oil, but there had been no wind, and they had managed to keep it from spreading. By the time Virgil and I had slept late and eaten breakfast, and had gone to survey things, Arrow Street had been cleaned up. The undertaker had done his job. The corpses were gone and there was nothing to see but the charred ruins of the church, from which, here and there, some smoke still rose. The remnants of Brother Percival were probably in there somewhere, but no one seemed interested in looking.

"Well," Virgil said, "let's go visit Pike. See how part two is going to play."

"No reason to wait," I said.

"None," Virgil said.

We walked up to the Palace and went in.

Choctaw was in the lookout chair, and Pike was having a later breakfast than we had, sitting near the bar. I stood against the wall with the eight-gauge where I could look at Choctaw and he could look at me. Virgil walked over to Pike.

"Virgil," Pike said. "Pull up a chair, my friend."

Virgil sat.

"Coffee?" Pike said

"Sure."

Pike gestured, and one of the bartenders brought coffee.

"You saw it all last night," Pike said.

"I did," Virgil said. "Me 'n Everett."

"So you know they attacked us," Pike said.

"Yep."

"Got a right to defend myself," Pike said.

Virgil nodded.

"Ain't mourning Percival," Virgil said.

Pike nodded and ate half a biscuit.

"Glad he done it himself," Pike said. "Otherwise, sooner or later, I was gonna have to do it."

"Worked out for you," Virgil said. "You pretty much got the town now."

Pike nodded and leaned back and sipped some coffee.

"Pretty much," he said after he swallowed.

" 'Cept for me 'n Everett," Virgil said.

" 'Cept for that," Pike said.

Virgil smiled. Pike smiled back. Choctaw was trying to keep an eye on me, and one on Virgil, which was hard because we were spread out. Which was why we were spread out.

"Wasn't gonna talk with you 'bout that quite so soon," Pike said. "But since it's come up . . . ?"

He shrugged.

Virgil shrugged back.

"I like you, Virgil," Pike said. "I really do."

"Everybody does," Virgil said.

Pike looked into his coffee cup for a while. Then he raised his eyes and looked at Virgil.

"I don't see how it's gonna work between us here," Pike said. "I don't see how you gonna let me run the town the way I want to."

"Don't see that myself," Virgil said.

"We ain't broke no law," Pike said.

"Might be able to find one," Virgil said.

"There's two of you," Pike said. "And there's twenty-five of us."

" 'Course, none of you is Virgil Cole," Virgil said. "Or Everett Hitch."

"Maybe, maybe not," Pike said. "But it's still twenty-five to two. And you got them women to think about."

"Good point," Virgil said. "You got a suggestion?"

"You could stop being deputies and work for me."

"Nope."

Pike nodded.

"Okay," he said. "I figured that you wouldn't. But you still got them women to think about. How about I give you some money? Enough to take care of them for a good while? I ain't even giving it to you. I'm giving it to you for them."

"What's the other option?" Virgil said.

"We gonna have to kill you and probably them," Pike said.

"Or at least try," Virgil said.

"I like our odds," Pike said. "And, God's honest truth, I think I can beat you."

Virgil was quiet, thinking about things. I knew Virgil didn't care if Pike thought he could beat him. Virgil paid no mind to talk.

After a time, he said, "Makes sense. I'll take the money . . . long as it is commensurate."

"And leave town?"

"And leave town," Virgil said.

"Your word?" Pike said.

"Yep."

Pike looked at me.

"Everett?" he said.

"I'm with Virgil," I said.

"Wait right there," Pike said.

He stood and went into the back of the saloon. He was gone for maybe ten minutes, and when he returned he had a leather-bound canvas satchel.

"One thousand dollars," he said. "Legal tender notes."

"Done," Virgil said.

He picked up the satchel and nodded at me, and we walked out of Pike's Palace.

63

"Virgil," I said, as we walked up Arrow Street, "what the fuck are we doing?"

"We're being tricky," Virgil said.

"We never took a bribe in our life," I said.

"Nor run away," Virgil said.

"So . . . ?" I said.

"We ain't going," Virgil said.

"We're not?"

"Nope."

"We're going to double-cross Pike?"

"We are," Virgil said.

"What about the bribe?"

"Laurel needs money," Virgil said. "Pike don't."

"You think Pike will see it that way?" I said.

"No."

"We gonna pretend to go?" I said.

"Yep."

"What about the women," I said.

"It was only Allie," Virgil said. "Maybe I

say she's a grown woman. She cast her lot with me. She knows what I do. . . . But the kid didn't get to cast her lot at all. It got cast for her. . . . And she ain't got no one else."

"And Pike would use them against us."

" 'Course he would," Virgil said. "You heard him."

I nodded.

"As I recall," I said, "Pike told us, 'You got them women to worry about.' "

"What I recall, too," Virgil said. "We stay, we'll be spending all our time protecting them. He needs to think they gone."

"So where we going to hide them," I said.

"Ain't figured that part out yet," Virgil said.

"What happens to them if we get killed?" I said.

"I thought 'bout that," Virgil said.

"And?"

"I can't worry 'bout that," he said. "I can't not be Virgil Cole."

"No," I said. "You can't."

Virgil grinned at me.

" 'Sides, we ain't never been killed yet," he said.

"Commensurate," I said, "with who we are."

"Commensurate," Virgil said.

"What about Pony?" I said.

"I'd guess he'll be with us," Virgil said.

"Maybe he could take the ladies some-place," I said.

Virgil nodded. We turned off of Arrow Street and walked toward where we'd been staying. Pony was on a bench on the front porch with Laurel beside him, and Allie was in a rocker, trying to sew a button on one of Virgil's shirts.

Virgil set the canvas satchel down and took a seat. I remained standing, leaning against one of the porch pillars. Virgil opened the satchel.

"Best thing I got to tell you is we got some money," he said.

64

Everyone was quiet while Virgil explained the situation.

When he was through, Allie said, "So why don't we all go? Find another town? Start over?"

"Can't do that," Virgil said.

"Why not? Not even you and Everett can fight Pike by yourselves. I mean, my God, he must have fifty men."

"Twenty-five," Virgil said.

"You want to stay and fight twenty-five men by yourself?"

"Me and Everett," Virgil said.

"Why? I mean, I know that you're Virgil Cole and all that. But why risk all our lives for it."

Virgil shook his head and didn't say anything.

"He run away," Pony said. "He man who run away."

Allie frowned, staring at Pony, then at Vir-

287

gil, as if she were working on a puzzle. Then she nodded slowly.

"Yes," she said.

"Here's what I been thinking," Virgil said. "We go down to the station in the morning. The four of us, and get on the train to Del Rio. We get out from town maybe five miles, that straight patch of the river where the train runs right along the bank. Pony's there with an extra horse. I get the train to stop. Me and Everett get off. Pony gets on. We ride back into town, sorta light-footed. Pony goes on to Del Rio. I'll write you a letter to give to Dave Morrissey down there, help you get settled. Then me and Everett will take care of business and come on down to join you."

"No," Allie said.

Virgil looked startled, which was an amazing thing to see, because Virgil never looked startled.

"No?" he said.

"Absolutely not," Allie said. "I won't leave you, and neither will Laurel."

Virgil looked at Laurel.

Laurel shook her head.

"Why not?" Virgil said.

"I won't," Allie said.

"Why not?" Virgil said.

"I'm a mess," Allie said. "I been a mess

long as you've known me. But I got this child to think 'bout now, and I can't keep being a mess."

Virgil looked at her and didn't answer. Virgil never looked puzzled, any more than he ever looked startled, but if he had he would have looked puzzled now.

"What kind of woman would leave her man at a time like this, to go hide, while he risked his life?"

Virgil shrugged and looked at me. I shrugged.

"That's right," she said, as if we had answered. "And I will not be that kind of woman anymore, not ever, anymore. I cannot be that kind of woman and be with this child . . . or you."

Virgil looked at me again.

"Sounds right to me," I said.

Virgil nodded.

"And I don't want Pony taking care of us," Allie said. "I want Pony to be with you."

"Who looks out for you and Laurel?" Virgil said.

"Me," Allie said.

"You?"

"I have a gun; I know how to shoot," Allie said. "You taught me."

Laurel stepped to Virgil's chair and whispered to him. He listened. He nodded.

"Okay," he said. "We don't go to Del Rio."

"We can pretend to," I said.

"And where do Allie and Laurel go?" Virgil said. "Ain't good tactics to leave them out for Pike."

"No," I said. "We need to hide them."

"Where?" Virgil said.

No one spoke for a moment, and then I said, "Lemme go talk to my friend Frisco."

"The whore?"

"Yes," I said.

"In Pike's Palace?" Virgil said.

"Where would he be less likely to look?" I said.

"I'll be back in an hour or so," I said.

"Take you that long?" Virgil said.

"No," I said. "But I might have to wait my turn."

Allie smiled at me.

"Not if I was Frisco," she said.

I said, "Thank you, Allie."

And I stood and walked back up toward Pike's Palace.

65

Frisco's room and place of employment was on the second floor at Pike's. But I went boldly in. I had till morning to leave town.

"Come for a good-bye poke," Frisco said when she let me in.

"Good-bye?" I said.

Frisco closed the door and locked it. We sat on her bed together.

"Heard you was leaving town tomorrow," she said.

"Word gets around," I said.

"Pike's telling everybody he run you and Virgil Cole out of town," she said.

"Proud of himself," I said.

"Yes," Frisco said.

She was wearing a short, thin nightgown and not much else.

"Before we get into farewells," I said, "I need a favor."

"You know me, Everett," Frisco said. "I only do the regular things. I don't do no specialties."

"None needed," I said. "I need to hide two women here, in this room, for a few hours tomorrow."

"Two women?"

"Yep."

"The ones with you and Virgil?" she said. "Allie and the kid, the one the Indian took?"

"Yes," I said.

I had no problem lying to her, but who else would it be?

"Her mother, what was her name?"

"Mary Beth," I said. "Mary Beth Oster-mueller."

"Yeah, her," Frisco said. "Killed herself two rooms down from here. Drunk, put a forty-five in her mouth and blew the top of her head off."

"I know," I said.

"Awful mess," Frisco said. "Pike was furious, but she was already dead, you know, so he couldn't kill her. Took a couple days to get that room cleaned up."

"Forty-five can make a big exit hole," I said.

"I guess," Frisco said. "Why'd she do that, anyway?"

"Life was too hard, I guess."

"That hard?"

"She and her daughter had a bad time of

292

it, 'fore we got them back."

"Daughter didn't kill herself."

"No," I said. "I think having her daughter watch what happened to her, and her having to watch while it happened to her daughter, right in front of her . . ."

Frisco nodded.

"Woman needed to be tougher," Frisco said.

"She did," I said. "And she wasn't."

"I take these two women in here," Frisco said, "and Pike finds out, what happens?"

"He'll kill them," I said. "And you."

"So why should I take the chance?" Frisco said.

" 'Cause we plan to kill him," I said. " 'Fore he finds out."

Frisco nodded.

"They can stay here; I'll move down with Big Red," she said. "You don't kill him, I'll claim I don't know how they got in here, but I come back and found the door locked and figured one of the other girls was using the room for business."

"Might work," I said.

"When they coming?"

"Tomorrow morning," I said. "You know Pony Flores?"

"No."

"Breed," I said. "Dark, kind of tall, works

some for Pike."

"Tall as you?"

"Nope," I said. "More like Virgil."

"High moccasins, knife in the top?" Frisco said.

"That's him," I said. "He'll bring them in the morning."

"Ain't normally very busy in the morning. They come in; I go out."

"Thank you," I said.

Frisco leaned her head against my shoulder.

"I'll miss you," she said. "You're a good guy."

"You too," I said.

"Want to do it 'fore you go?" she said.

"I would," I said.

Frisco grinned and patted my crotch.

"I could tell," she said.

66

In the morning, Virgil and I walked with Allie and Laurel down to the train station and got aboard the nine-o'clock train to Del Rio. Allie carried a carpetbag. Virgil and I just had weapons and ammunition. The train left the station on time, and when we were under way, Virgil got up and spoke with the conductor. The conductor shook his head and Virgil tapped the deputy star on his shirt and spoke again. The conductor looked at us and paused, then nodded, and moved on, toward the front of the train.

Virgil came back and sat, on the aisle, with his right hand free, where he could look at the door at the front of the car. I sat opposite, with the eight-gauge beside me, where I could look at the back door, same as we always did. We didn't speak of it, we did it automatically, the way we always spread apart approaching a fight or entering a strange place. We'd been doing what we did for so long that sometimes we seemed to me like two parts of the same apparatus.

As the train came in close to the river, I could feel it begin to slow, and about a half-mile into the straightaway, it braked and came to a sort of muttering halt the way trains do. We stood and got off the train. Pony was there, with four saddle horses. The horses were grazing comfortably on tether. We walked to the horses, and the train started up and moved south with slowly increasing speed.

We got the women mounted without saying anything.

"You know how you're going to get them into Frisco's room," Virgil said.

Pony nodded.

"Know all parts of Pike's Palace," Pony said.

"Including the whores' quarters," Virgil said.

"Them 'specially, jefe," he said.

"You got the gun I gave you," Virgil said to Allie.

"In my bag," she said.

"And bullets," Virgil said.

Allie nodded and patted the carpetbag that hung on her saddle horn.

"And you'll stay in there and be quiet no matter what," Virgil said.

"Yes."

Pony pulled his horse up next to Laurel. He took a .45 derringer out of his coat pocket, broke it open. Took out the two bullets, closed it again.

"Chiquita," Pony said.

He held the gun out and cocked it.

"Click," Pony said.

He pulled the trigger.

"Bang," he said.

He cocked it again and pulled the trigger again.

"Click," he said. "Bang."

Laurel nodded.

"Do that?" Pony said, and handed her the gun.

She cocked it.

Pony nodded and said, "Click."

She pulled the trigger.

Pony said, "Bang."

She nodded and dry-fired it again. Then she gave the gun back to Pony. He loaded it.

"Now," Pony said. "Click-bang only when you mean it."

He pointed to the middle of his body.

"Shoot here," he said.

Laurel nodded.

"Shoot only to protect yourself," I said.

She nodded and put the gun in her coat pocket.

Virgil said, "You get them settled, Pony."

"Sí."

"Nobody sees them."

"Sí."

"We'll be along in the afternoon. We see you in the saloon, we know it's all gone right."

Pony nodded and turned his horse and rode a little way toward town, and paused and waited for the women.

Allie paused and looked at Virgil.

"I love you," she said.

Virgil nodded.

Laurel pulled her horse close to him and bent down from the saddle and whispered to him.

He nodded.

"Me 'n Everett been doing this most of our lives," Virgil said. "We know how."

We all sat silently for a moment.

"You come back to us," Allie said.

"We will," Virgil said.

Then he pointed toward Pony and gave Allie's horse a slap on the flank. The horse moved forward and Laurel's followed, and they rode away from us, toward town.

67

Virgil and I sat on the riverbank and waited for Pony to do what he needed to.

"I don't know if we're really smart or really dumb," I said, "hiding the women upstairs at Pike's."

"Nobody goes up there but whores and customers," Virgil said. "Pony told me employees ain't allowed."

"Pike sure as hell wouldn't look for them there."

"No," Virgil said.

A fish splashed in the river and left a series of concentric ripples. Bass probably, snapping up a dragonfly.

"Why is it exactly that we're going to kill him?" I said.

"That what we going to do?" Virgil said.

" 'Course it is," I said. " 'Less he kills us."

"Just want to talk with Pike," Virgil said.

"Horseshit," I said. "You took his money and double-crossed him, and now you're gonna go and shove it in his face. You know he is gonna have to pull on you."

Virgil smiled.

"I do," Virgil said.

"Maybe what we doing ain't quite exactly law-officer business anyway," I said.

"Must be," Virgil said. "We're law officers."

"Some folks might say we should have stepped in between Percival and Pike," I said.

"You miss Percival?"

"Nope."

"He was a fraud," Virgil said. "He was in cahoots with Pike to drive out all of Pike's competition. He messed with Laurel. He messed with Allie. He give Allie to Pike."

"At least that's how she saw it," I said.

Virgil looked at me for a time.

"Allie is Allie," he said. "You gonna miss Pike?"

"Might have saved a lot of trouble if he'd told us all he knew 'bout Buffalo Calf," I said.

"Might have," Virgil said.

"So, is it tactics?" I said. "Let the vermin fight to the death and then pick off the winner?"

"Sure," Virgil said.

"Or is it personal?" I said. " 'Cause of

Laurel and Allie . . . maybe Mary Beth?"

"Sure," Virgil said.

"So you're feeling all right 'bout this business," I said.

"We not gonna back-shoot anybody," Virgil said. "We risk our lives to do what we think, the right thing to do. Somebody told me once that was pretty much all you could ask for."

"Who was that?" I said.

"A smart fella," Virgil said, and sipped some coffee. "Went to West Point."

"Oh," I said. "Him."

The resident bass, or whatever it was, jumped for another dragonfly, or whatever it was, and left the circles of his jump on the surface of the water. We both watched the ripples as they widened slowly out until they disappeared against the riverbank.

"When we're finished with Pike," I said, "what you gonna do with Allie?"

"Gonna keep her," Virgil said.

"You think she's changed?" I said.

"I think she has," Virgil said.

I didn't say anything.

"You think she has?" Virgil said.

"Don't know," I said.

"It's the girl," Virgil said. "I see her with the girl and I see a different Allie."

"Maybe," I said.

"People change," Virgil said.

"Not a lot of them," I said.

Virgil was silent for a moment.

Then he said, "No, not a lot of them.

"Somebody got to take care of Laurel," Virgil said.

"That would be Allie," I said.

"That would be Allie," Virgil said.

"Guess the question's settled for the moment," I said.

"I guess," Virgil said.

68

Virgil and I walked up Arrow Street toward Pike's Palace in the early afternoon. The day was bright. There was a pleasant breeze off the river. Virgil was wearing his Colt and carrying a Winchester in his left hand. I had my Colt and the eight-gauge.

"You got a plan?" I said.

"I do," Virgil said. "I figure we'll walk into Pike's and see what happens."

"That's a plan?" I said.

"Sure," Virgil said.

"Walk in cold against twenty-five men?" I said.

"We get Pike early, there won't be twenty-five. They'll fade like a spring blossom. Probably won't be that many in there this hour of the day, anyway."

I paused in front of a sign nailed to one of the overhang supports on the boardwalk in front of a hardware shop.

"No guns to be carried in Brimstone

without permission," the sign read. It was signed "Chauncey Brown, Town Marshal."

"Chauncey Brown?" I said.

"That'd be Choctaw," Virgil said.

"So quick," I said.

"Pike's like me," Virgil said. "Needs to be done, may as well get to it."

We arrived in front of Pike's Palace. There was another one of Choctaw's signs outside the door. We stood for a minute. I cocked the eight-gauge.

Then I said, "Here we go."

Virgil winked at me, and we went in. I went to the corner to the right of the door where I could see the whole room. Virgil went past me and walked around the bar so he was away from me.

"Afternoon," Virgil said to the bartender. "Could you tell Pike that Virgil Cole would like to see him."

The bartender jerked his head up when Virgil spoke, and stared at him.

Then he said, "Yes sir," and walked fast toward the back of the room. Across the room I could see Pony Flores having a meal alone at a table. When he saw us he stood and leaned against the wall. No one paid any attention. Nothing happened for a while. Then Abner came out of the back of the saloon carrying his lookout sawed-off.

Some of Pike's other gun hands appeared and began to spread out around the room. I stayed where I was. Pony stood against the far wall, and Virgil seemed comfortable and at peace, standing by the bar.

It was maybe twenty more minutes before Pike appeared, walking easily from the back, wearing a Colt.

"Virgil Cole," he said pleasantly, "you cocksucker, why are you here?"

"Val Verde County deputy sheriffs," Virgil said.

"For what?"

"Being a really bad asshole," Virgil said.

"You think those badges mean you can take my money and double-cross me?" Pike said. "I bought them badges, and you. And you took the money and double-crossed me."

"We left town like we promised," Virgil said. "We didn't say nothing about not coming back."

"Virgil," Pike said, as if he was tired, "don't fuck with me. You know and I know that I'm gonna have to kill the both of you."

"Sorry you feel that way, Pike," Virgil said.

I wondered where Choctaw was. He'd been hired for this kind of moment. But I couldn't look for him. If the ball went up, I needed to be focused. I had to kill Abner with one barrel, and maybe clean out a couple more with the other barrel. If the dance started, Choctaw would announce himself.

Virgil was silent, waiting. In the saloon, people began to scramble for cover. It was helpful in sorting out who were shooters and who were not. Pike continued to look at Virgil. They were maybe six feet apart. I didn't know if Pike was cranking up his courage or savoring his moment. Virgil was simply waiting. The saloon wasn't crowded this time of day. The spectators' scrambling stopped as all of them got out of the way. The room was quiet. The tension in the room was like a physical pressure.

Then Pike said very clearly, "I believe I can beat you," and moved a step away from Virgil.

Upstairs somebody fired some shots, maybe three, and the tension exploded. Abner half turned at the sound and I shot him with one barrel, and the two gunmen to his right with the other barrel. Pony shot two men from the far side of the room. Something tumbled from the upstairs balcony. And Pike found he couldn't beat Virgil.

Pike was good. He had his gun in his hand. He'd cleared leather. But the gun was pointing at the floor and Pike was taking a step backward, then another. Then he suddenly went down and lay on his back on the floor with his mouth open and blood soaking into his shirt front.

When Pike went down, everything stopped.

Virgil stood still by the bar with his Colt in his hand. I was flattened against the wall with my Colt out, and Pony stood across in a crouch, with his weapon out and another Colt stuck in his waistband. The room buzzed with silence.

"We got you from three corners," Virgil said. "And we can shoot. You want to stay with this, we'll kill you. And with Pike gone, what is there to die for?"

The remainder of Pike's crew stood uncertainly. They had their hands near their guns, but none of them had drawn.

"You leave them weapons in the holsters," Virgil said. "And get out of here and keep going, you gonna live. I see you again and I'll kill you."

One of the men said, "I'm leaving," and with his gun holstered walked out of the room. In a moment three others went after him. Virgil watched them go, then walked slowly around the room.

"Since Marshal Choctaw said nobody can wear guns, the only ones who'd be wearing one now," Virgil said, "would be Pike's people."

He moved from person to person. Pony and I held position.

"So I figure you got a gun, you're with Pike, and you want to use it," Virgil said.

Two men sitting in the back stood suddenly. Virgil turned easily toward them. One of the men put his hands up.

"We was with Pike," he said. "But we don't want no trouble."

Virgil nodded and pointed toward the door. Both men walked out. There were no other guns in the room. When he got through looking, Virgil went and glanced at what had fallen from the balcony. It was a Winchester. He looked up and Choctaw was there, head down, half over the balcony railing. Virgil studied him for a moment.

Then he said, "Allie?"

There was a sudden tumble of footsteps from the balcony, and Allie came running down the stairs with Laurel behind her. Allie was carrying the short Colt that Virgil had given her. She kept on coming when she reached the saloon and lunged against Virgil, with Laurel right behind her.

Very gracefully, Virgil took the gun from her hand as she embraced him. He handed the gun to me, as Laurel embraced him, too. Virgil, looking a little embarrassed, put an arm around each of them. I looked up at the balcony. Frisco was standing there, looking down. She smiled and nodded. I nodded back.

Pony reloaded and holstered his weapon. I reloaded the eight-gauge and the short Colt that Allie had used. Despite an arm around each woman, Virgil was putting a fresh shell into his Colt, working carefully behind their heads. I smiled to myself.

Pony walked over to me.

"Just 'cause you can shoot," I said, "don't mean I want to hug you."

"No hug?" he said.

"No," I said.

Pony grinned.

"Good," he said.

69

The sign outside our office read CHAUNCEY BROWN, TOWN MARSHAL. We went in, Virgil, the women, Pony, and me. I got a hammer and knocked the marshal sign off, and went back in.

Virgil looked at Allie and smiled.

"So that's where Choctaw was," he said.

"He was fixin' to shoot you," Allie said.

Virgil nodded.

"They was all fixin' to shoot us," Virgil said. "Tell me about Choctaw."

Laurel was sitting beside Allie on the couch. She was looking at Allie and at Virgil, and sometimes at Pony and at me. She sat perfectly still. She was still silent, but it was, somehow, a lively silence, as if she wanted to jump around.

"Well . . ." Allie said.

Allie's stories were often long. If you asked her what was for supper, she'd start with when she went for groceries yesterday. But

Virgil didn't push her.

"Pony brought us into town, and we snuck up the back outside stairs and no one paid us no mind. Anybody saw us probably figured we was just some whores coming to work."

She looked at Pony and smiled.

"With a customer," she said.

Virgil nodded.

"And Frisco let us in, and said she'd go down the hall and stay with another whore and we could have the room to ourselves. It was a nice room for a whore. I mean, some of the rooms I've . . ."

She stopped.

"Anyway, Pony left us and said he'd be downstairs in the saloon, and he went and we locked the door and I took out the gun you gave me, and we both went and watched out the window till we seen you ride into town. Then, a'course, we both run to the door to listen, see what was going to happen."

As she talked, I stood in the doorway and kept an eye on the street. I saw the undertaker's wagon go by, headed for Pike's Palace. Otherwise, everything was quiet.

"And all of a sudden we hear men talking right outside the door. And one of them, I think it was Mr. Pike, one of them says, 'You can't find the women?' And the other one says, 'They ain't at the house.' And the first one, I'm sure it's Mr. Pike, says, 'He took them or he hid them. We'll find them after we get through with Cole.' "

Virgil sat in his chair, perfectly still, listening. Pony stood and got a dipper of water and drank.

"Well," Allie said, "you can imagine how we felt. But we're listening and listening. And Choctaw says to Pike, 'How many are they,' and Mr. Pike says, 'Two.' And Choctaw says, 'Cole and Hitch?' And Mr. Pike says, 'Yes.' And Choctaw says, 'They that good?' And Pike says, 'Don't matter how good they are, 'cause you're gonna be up here with a Winchester.' "

Allie was having a good time. She paused now, and looked at all of us.

"And Choctaw says, 'How you want it to go?' And Mr. Pike says, 'You get him in your sights and when I say I believe I can beat you, I'll step aside and you kill him.' Well, let me tell you," Allie said, "my blood 'bout froze when he said that. And Choctaw says, 'Kill Cole first?' and Pike says, 'Yes, then Hitch.' And Choctaw says, 'Everybody else in place?' And Mr. Pike says, 'Yes, got eight guns in the room, including Abner.' And then they're quiet, and I hear them moving

312

around outside my door, and then Mr. Pike says, 'See him?' And Choctaw says, 'Got him.' Then Mr. Pike says, 'Okay.' And I hear him walk away."

Laurel, sill wordless and not moving, somehow radiated excitement. She leaned suddenly toward Allie and made a rolling motion with her hands. Allie nodded and smiled at her. Pony drank some more water. Virgil never moved. I looked back up the street. The undertaker's wagon was no longer in sight.

"So," Allie said, making the small word sound long. "I put on the chain bolt and I peek out, and there he is, five feet away, behind one of the drapes, with a rifle. So I aim at him, and I wait. And I can hear your voice and Mr. Pike's, and I wait and then I hear Pike say, 'I believe . . .' And Choctaw steps out from behind the drape and I shot him in the middle of the back, like you told me, aim for the middle, and Choctaw doubles backwards and snaps forward, and the rifle falls over the balcony and he falls on the railing, and then everybody downstairs starts shooting and I slammed the door and locked it, and then I heard you call me. And I opened it and we came down and . . ."

"I know the rest," Virgil said quietly.

"Yes," Allie said. "Of course you do."

70

"I need to know one thing," Allie said.

She seemed still caught up in the drama of the recitation.

"How did you know it was me?"

"Had to be," Virgil said. "Wasn't no one else it coulda been."

Allie smiled and nodded.

"Actually, two things," Allie said. "I want to know if I hadn't shot him, would he have killed you."

Virgil nodded.

"Probably would have," Virgil said.

"And Everett?"

"Maybe," Virgil said.

"So that means I saved your life," Allie said.

"It does," Virgil said.

"And Everett?" she said.

"Yes, ma'am," I said. "And I'm grateful."

She nodded as if she was satisfied.

"Does that, maybe a little bit, anyway,"

Allie said, "make up for any of the bad things?"

Virgil grinned at her.

"Yes," he said. "It does."

I went to the desk and took out a bottle. Then I got some coffee cups and poured all of us, including Laurel, a drink. I made Laurel's drink short. Then I handed the cups out. I raised my cup, and everyone raised theirs. We drank. No one said anything.

Then Allie said, "What are we going to do now? Are we going to stay here?"

"Not good memories here," Virgil said, and nodded at Laurel.

"No," Allie said. "We should go someplace else."

Virgil looked at me.

"Everett?" he said.

"Agree," I said. "We should move on."

"I'll telegram Morrissey," Virgil said. "Tell him we're quitting."

I nodded. We drank a little more whiskey, except for Laurel.

"Where?" Allie said.

"Where what?" Virgil said.

"Where are we going to go?" Allie said.

"Hadn't thought about it," Virgil said.

"I want to start over," Allie said.

"Okay," Virgil said.

"I want to go back to Appaloosa," Allie said. "Close the circle. Begin again, see if we can do better . . . see if I can do better."

"Everett?" Virgil said.

"Got no problem with Appaloosa," I said. "Maybe even got work for a couple of upstanding shootists like us."

Virgil nodded.

"Most places do," Virgil said.

"Ain't that fortunate," I said.

"We got the money from Pike," Virgil said. "We ain't pressed."

"Still gotta work," I said.

"Yes," Virgil said. "We do."

Virgil looked at the girl.

"Laurel?" Virgil said.

Laurel nodded and stepped close to him and whispered. Then she sat back down on the couch next to Allie.

"Laurel would be happy to visit Appaloosa," Virgil said. "Allie been tellin' her about it."

"So, maybe it ain't a sudden idea," I said. "That Allie just thought up."

Allie smiled faintly and said nothing.

Virgil said, "Maybe not."

"So, it's Appaloosa?" I said.

"It is," Virgil said. "You want to ride along, Pony?"

Pony shook his head.

"Where are you going?" Allie said.

"Mother's people," Pony said. "Live Chiricahua for a while. Living white face too hard."

Pony turned to Virgil.

"Jefe," he said.

And he put out his hand. Despite the fact that Virgil never shook hands, Virgil shook it.

"Pony," Virgil said.

Pony and I shook hands.

He nodded to Allie.

"Allie?" he said.

"We will miss you," Allie said.

Pony looked at Laurel.

"Chiquita," he said.

Laurel stood and took the derringer out of her coat pocket and handed it to Pony.

Pony shook his head.

"You keep," he said. "Remember Pony Flores."

She stared at him for a minute and then nodded and put it back in her pocket. Then she went to him and put her arms around him and hugged him for a long time.

Pony made no attempt to get loose. He stood quietly, patting her back between the shoulder blades. Then finally he took her arms gently and freed himself and guided her to the couch.

"Pony Flores come back someday, chiquita," he said, bending to look in her eyes. "You see Pony again."

She nodded.

Pony looked once more at Virgil. Virgil nodded. Pony nodded back. Then he turned and walked out of the office. We all sat silently, listening to the sound of Pony's horse as he rode away.

71

The stallion was still there, a gray leopard Appaloosa, tending his mares on the flank of a hill outside Appaloosa. He'd been there when I'd come to Appaloosa, and I'd passed him the last time I rode out. Now returning, I paused at the top of the hill to watch him. Virgil and the women went ahead, trailing the pack mule. The stallion reared and snorted at the scent of the mule, though the mule was no threat to his harem. One of the mares drifted away from the herd, and the stallion, glancing at me every few steps, moved off to get her and drive her back. When he got her back to the herd, he left her and came around to put himself between me and the mares. The wandering mare went right off again, not in a hurry, just like she had a mind of her own and wanted to graze where she wanted to graze. The stallion stood, stiff-legged, ears forward, looking at her. He bugled once. Then he looked at me and went after her again. This time he nipped her as he drove her back. She tried to kick him, but he was an old hand at this, and he evaded the kick without effort. He drove her to my side of the herd this time and pressed her in among the other mares. Then he resumed his position between me and the mares, cropping the grass, raising his head every few crops to check on my position. The mare began to edge her way through the other mares, away from the stud. He raised his head and looked at her and bugled again and hurried around to the other side of the herd to block her. She stopped, still among the other mares, and put her head down and began to graze. Eyeing me all the time now, he reluctantly stayed on that side of the herd. Several of the mares appeared to be carrying foals. After they were born, there would be wolves to deal with. Being a stallion is high-pressure business. I decided not to add to the pressure by hanging around, and turned my gelding down the slope and followed Virgil and the women on into Appaloosa.

ABOUT THE AUTHOR

Robert B. Parker has long been acknowledged as the dean of American crime fiction. His novels featuring the wise-cracking, street-smart Boston private-eye Spenser have earned him a devoted following and reams of critical acclaim. Robert Parker's most recent bestsellers include his Spenser novel, *Rough Weather*, and his Jesse Stone series.